December 28

THE EYES AROUND ME

THE
EYES
AROUND
ME

BY GAVIN BLACK

HARPER & ROW, PUBLISHERS

New York and Evanston

To Rena and Peter Barker,
with thanks

1

Ella Bain had started to put on weight after her first marriage and stopped only because she got a fright one day looking down her own front. Mirrors didn't do it, Ella said; it was looking down and not being able to see your feet which triggered off the panic. Now, as a result of terrible orgies of cutting out all starches when she should have been cutting out whisky, she could see her feet again. And long pointed shoes helped.

Ella was a Scots redhead, a pink girl, with corrugated ginger hair that maddened her so much she had once shaved it off to wear a tight black wig in which she looked like a pink girl wearing a black wig. Also, her own hair fighting back had prickled, so she had gone around for months in a bandana while things happened underneath. The eventual unveiling had revealed the ginger corrugations in a stronger than ever comeback.

Ella in a bathing suit looked like a Rubens type about to burst out of elasticized nylon. She liked green, which she claimed matched her eyes, which were not green, but a kind of tawny brown flecked with gray, and huge. She had the eyes of some aquatic mammal, damp and lustrous with desire.

Ella could never quite accept the fact that when she came into a room full of good-looking women the men started twitching away toward her. Ella said it was the Bain short-bread money that shouted from her diamonds, but it wasn't; she was as invincibly attractive as a sportive dolphin. Even women felt this, at least at first, until they found out that their males weren't just snorting in fun.

"What's the use of being born to a solid-gold spoon when you look like me?" Ella said, refusing to believe that to the right man she would have been splendor and joy. The right man, I was quite sure, would even have been able to slow down the boozing which had run in the Bain family from the master baker who could be said to have founded the line.

Between Eric, her first husband, and Miguel da Conti, her second, Ella had proposed to me, saying that with her money and my money we ought to be able to hold up the advance south of Mao Tse-tung, but I was too busy at the time to contemplate a future on this grand scale. Which is not to say that I didn't love Ella; I did. It was sad that she couldn't really believe so many of us did love her. She saw herself as doomed forever to move in the unnerving opulence provided by the increasing international sale of Scots biscuits.

Ella had a big house in the Dundee luxe suburb of Broughty Ferry to which she swept back every second year wearing sables out of storage in London and a pink sunburn. She spent three weeks shivering, during which time she showed everyone that baking ran in her blood, even though this might be thinned out by the tropics and alcohol. Business always looked up after Ella's visits, and there was usually a new product for the U.S. market like tinned woodcock baked in heather honey and encased in whisky-impregnated Bain dough, at seventeen dollars a time.

Of her husbands, Eric was a mistake which had lasted seven years, and Miguel was another which lasted two. Eric was a Colonial civil servant, a determined careerist putting up a fight for survival in an Empire so much reduced that there was scarcely standing room left for him and his rivals. And though

2

Ella's money should have been a great help, it somehow wasn't, for there was Ella herself. Her idea of a party was something which ended naturally when the neighbors called in the police.

Miguel had perhaps been an understandable reaction to living with a man who has a purpose. Miguel had no purpose except Ella's money. However, she was Scots about this; she didn't mind throwing it about on occasion, but later on got out her little red notebook and jotted down the outlays for dissipation. Miguel just had no opportunities for graft at all.

Ella was a sad girl, with a lot of love to offer, and men standing around who for various reasons couldn't take it.

"You want to be reminded of death all the time in life," Ella said. "That's why I built my house in Hong Kong."

She had brought Yamabushi down from Tokyo to build it for her on the south shore of the island. Yamabushi's fee was reported to be thirty thousand Hong Kong dollars. What the house had cost I couldn't guess. It was one of those natural growths in concrete lumps out of a rock face, and in a typhoon a wave had taken most of the garden, so Ella decided not to have a garden at all and kept her three Chinese hired men digging up any weeds that had survived the salt.

On Hogmanay in Hong Kong, in Archie MacAndrew's house, Ella was a Scots queen of love. It didn't matter, because the party was eighty percent Scots, too, and the other twenty percent of mixed English and Chinese had come along in a tolerant mood to watch the savages at their annual rites.

Ella was doing an eightsome in the way it should be done. The dance needs lassies with a bit of meat on them and moving parts. Opposite her was a skeletal Chinese called Wong, who had studied law at Edinburgh University and made good use of his spare time with the natives. The others in the set were just supporting players while Wong was spun by Ella, an elfin smile staying fixed on his old-young face.

"Hough!" Ella shouted.

"Hough!" Wong echoed.

He was doing the authentic prance of the male, light-footed but muscled, and no ballet movement. Ella came at him like a dreadnought, but he never flinched.

"Man, we could be in Kilspindie," Archie said, taking my arm. "Come and have a drink."

He had thoughtfully provided a bar between some arches of his discreetly palatial Peak residence and sent the servants to bed before there was any danger of them seeing things that mightn't help the white man's prestige out East. We're all rather touchy about this kind of thing these days, watching our images, not exactly Peace Corps boys maybe, but still making a point of not throwing away, in public, cigars that haven't been smoked down to the butt. Archie had a particularly fine image to keep up and spent a large part of each day doing it.

"When I give you the sign," Archie said, "will you break up the party by taking Ella away? I've got a surgery at ten tomorrow. Drag her out by the hair if you have to. Or tell her you want to first-foot."

"I don't."

"We're getting old, that's the trouble. No bashing on people's doors at two in the morning. Well, well. I can mind when things was different for you and me."

"When you lapse into Scots, Archie, the mask slips."

"What mask?"

"Your Hong Kong Harley Street mask. Ten-dollars-a-minute MacAndrew."

"Are you saying I'm a crook?"

"No, you're a damn good doctor. You might even be worth the three dollars a minute you'd get anywhere else."

He looked at me over his glass.

"What's the swindle that brought you up here?"

"I came to get money."

"I thought you were stuffed with it?"

"I'm trying to finance a new company. Only a fool uses his own money on that kind of project. There's a lot of Trengganu silver waiting to be mined and the price these days makes it an interesting proposition."

"But why Hong Kong? Have the Singapore oil-palm kings got wise to you?"

"There's more floating capital up here. Plenty of your Chinese are looking for a featherbed to land on when Hong Kong goes back to the motherland."

"This place will last a long time yet."

"That's what they said in Shanghai."

"Here, Paul, look down at the city. New skyscrapers."

"They had them in Shanghai, too. They're still there."

"So we've asked a Jonah for the New Year? If that's your mood, keep away from Louise. It's her mood, too."

"What's my mood, dear?" Louise said behind us.

Louise was one of the twenty percent who weren't Scots. She looked as though she came out of an English rectory garden straight from snipping things in the borders. She was a blonde who had kept her looks out East while her husband lost a good deal of his hair. She believed, along with being an Anglican, in reincarnation, and had told me once she was being punished now for having wasted her gifts in another life. She played the piano competently, painted in water colors, and wrote little stories about living in the Orient for an English magazine that was still published despite the fact it seemed designed for nursery governesses. People said they were fond of Louise even though she was so often a breath of sanity just when you didn't want one. Like tonight. She drifted around her husband's party being charmingly sane about the guests, and somehow that wasn't as endearing as it ought to be.

"What's my mood, Archie?"

His face tightened, as though a key had been turned two or three times.

"I just meant that you get a bit depressed about this place." Louise looked at me.

"It has no feel of permanence, Paul. I sense that particularly when I'm painting. I do a lot from the terrace here. And do you know what I always have to put in first? The blue hills of China. They're permanent."

Having given me this thought Louise turned toward the well-heeled peasants making all that row, staring at them, trying to understand, but failing. Finally she said with a certain plaintiveness, "Isn't there going to be any ordinary dancing?"

Ella was coming toward us with an arm about Wong's shoulders. She stopped and kissed him on the cheek. "My brave wee mannie." Then she pushed him toward the bar.

"Did you see us?" Ella asked. "I'm sending home for a kilt for Wong. He must have a kilt."

Wong's smile was fixed on his face.

"I have knees as smooth as a dancing girl's," he said.

A couple of hours later I tracked Ella down to the terrace. She had lost Wong and was sitting with a major in a garrison regiment who looked happy in the way of those who have never put any strain on their twelve-year-old intelligences.

It was cold outside and the flesh revealed by Ella's plunge neckline should have been goose pimpled, but it wasn't. The major must have switched on the ship's light; Ella would never have done it.

"Darling, this is Harry Arbuthnot. Paul Harris."

The major was certain he had heard of me, something in the papers. Ella suggested a police notice. But the major said no, it was something about business which was odd, what?, because he never bothered about that sort of thing much. It was a good thing he hadn't tried business; he'd have starved. I had seen Ella going to some curious lengths in her pursuit of the male, but this seemed to me scraping the bottom of the barrel.

Arbuthnot took a deep breath.

"You know," he said. "Tonight's party has made me feel that Scotland must be enormously jolly. It's so odd that I've never got up there. Even to shoot. Are you Scots, Mr. Harris?"

"Yes."

Ella giggled. "He's a liar. He was born in the jungle and never knew his parents."

When I had Ella on the floor inside for some ordinary dancing I said, "You're not doing a line with the military, are you?"

"They're sweet. You keep thinking there can't be anything like that left, and then you stumble on a whole regiment full. I give them drinks. It's part of seeing the Orient. And they're always free when everyone else is working. It keeps my house beautifully noisy."

"We're going home now," I said.

"It's only one o'clock!"

"Louise is yawning."

She came quietly, which rather surprised me. We started the movement out, Ella coming slowly down a wide stairway wearing what looked like a quarter of an acre of Manchurian ocelot for the cold weather. She kissed Louise.

"You must come to dinner," Louise said, squeezing my hand. Then, very softly, "On your own, if you like."

"Happy New Year!" Archie shouted after us.

Ella turned and waved to him. Then she said, "He's getting awfully middle-aged, poor Archie. But what can you expect with a wife who talks to him about the garden at breakfast? You drive."

"Believe me, I'm going to."

"Take the road over the Peak."

Ella's car was a mini-Morris, not hotted up at all, good enough for the island, she said, though it sat in her three-place garage like a perambulator someone had forgotten about. It wasn't easy for her to get in and out of, either. Most of her coat got in first, and she was still doing a sort of contortionist act in the seat beside me, struggling with ocelot, when I had reached third gear.

The Peak is like any town's executive suburb except that, where these are most often on the flat side, this one has the feel of something pushed up from behind in a vast cataclysm which the residences have managed to survive. All those lovely homes ought to have fallen down on top of the skyscrapers long ago, but they haven't; and the higher you go the bigger the places become, which makes everything seem even more top-heavy. Archie's house wasn't quite tycoon level but we still had to come down from it to one of the bigger roads, and at a bend there was all Hong Kong and the harbor and even Kowloon below, with nobody planning to go to bed at all, the lights pain-hard in the cold air. A huge cruise liner had come in at the wrong season and was lying in the roads, its illumination pinker than anyone else's, two funnels spotlighted in a boudoir glow to suggest all that gaiety going on down underneath when you knew perfectly well that it was packed out with rich dyspeptics under sedation.

"I'm stone cold sober," Ella said.

"Well?"

"It's not like the New Year at all. We should have had a party at my house. But all I can think of now is to get out of the place. God, how I hate it! Why didn't you stop me building the thing?"

"I wasn't here."

"I wrote you about it. I even phoned you. And all you said was to do what I thought best. You ought to know by this time that's never any good."

"What's on your mind?" I asked.

"Everything's a mess, Paul."

"Let's get down to specifics."

"Well . . . one of them is Angus. He's here."

I was surprised.

"In Hong Kong?"

"Yes. For more than a year."

"And you never mentioned him in your letters? Or phone calls?"

"Well . . . you've never exactly taken to Angus. No one does."

"He's not really your problem."

"He's my brother!"

"Oh. You're feeling like that?"

"Paul, I got him out here. I mean I'm responsible. I wrote him about the refugees over in Kowloon. He was between charities and so he flew out."

I had met Ella's half brother three times and liked him less on each occasion. His father had cut him out of the family will, severing him from baking, but he had sued under Scots law for his legal rights, and Bain's Limited had finally bought Angus off with a hundred thousand pounds. He had then proceeded to cultivate his conscience with good works, which were all right in themselves, indeed, fine; it was just something in the way he went about it, the boy at the end of the capitalist era spreading his riches from guilt. I wasn't sure, either, that he spread his riches so much. He was ten years younger than Ella but even at twenty-five went around with a kind of adolescent beatnik anger at everything but himself. Toward his sister he showed only an acid sarcasm which was totally without love, and perhaps I resented him because I couldn't like people who rejected Ella.

"Why isn't he staying with you?"

"In the sodden decadence of my house? Darling! He has a hut in a settlement. When he does come to see me he hasn't shaved for three days. Or washed. Oh . . . I shouldn't talk like this. I've seen what he's doing. It ought to be done, God knows. Archie has a clinic over there."

"In Kowloon? For good works?"

"We never know our friends, do we, darling? He keeps it very hush-hush. Maybe because Louise would think it was insanitary. She thinks we suffer now for what we were a couple of thousand years ago. And that goes for refugees, too.

9

Comforting, isn't it? The answer to so many problems. What do you think I was a couple of thousand years ago?"

I laughed.

Ella laughed, too.

"Oh, Paul, I love you. And it's pure. You've kept it that way."

We had reached a part of the Peak which gets the winds and isn't so expensive. The houses here were crowded, old ones with new ones in their gardens and these concrete boxes whose architects had never got over a bad attack of Le Corbusier. The poor were packed into Hong Kong, but so were the relatively rich.

"Stop the car, Paul!"

I had held her head as she leaned over a wall before this, so I got out, too. Ella wasn't leaning on anything; she was standing waiting.

"Come on," she said softly. "It's New Year. And we haven't first-footed anybody."

"The town's still up, but not the suburbs."

"Friends of mine here."

There was a steep curving drive with gates, and a bluster of trees masking a small garden, a place trying to look more impressive than it really was. Ella crossed the road, her heels clicking, and went through the gate.

"There's no light," I said.

"The sitting room's at the back."

"I'm not in the mood."

"Getting middle-aged, too, darling?"

She began to climb steps. I followed with a sullen vision of the kind of conviviality likely to be waiting, probably some service type and his wife who would rally from the first shock to emit the necessary squeaks of welcome and go for the gin bottle. If they were in bed they'd get out of it, responding to a terrible duty to be gay which is part of the code they live by.

You can't say no in the services; the people at the door may be friends of your commanding officer.

When I got to the door Ella had already pressed the bell.

"There's a ball at one of the hotels. These people may be at it, Ella."

"Oh, no, they won't."

She pressed again. A light came on in the way a light does in a house which has been closed down for the night, suggesting alarm and possibly even panic. Eventually there were shuffling sounds behind the door.

The man who opened it was decidedly tousled, in pajamas with a dressing gown over them. His hair, which wasn't luxuriant, was standing straight up, giving an odd pixie comment to a face that had grown the way it was from twenty years of taking its responsibilities very seriously indeed. The man staring at us was Eric Hisling, Ella's first husband.

"Good God!" he said.

"Happy New Year, darling."

"What? Now look here, Ella, what the devil . . ."

"We were passing, darling. And saw a light."

"You did *not* see a light. I'm damned if you saw a light!"

"Well, Paul thought he saw a light. Didn't you, darling? Anyway, you shouldn't be in bed. Not tonight."

"Who is it, Eric?" a distraught female voice called from a landing somewhere behind.

The man half turned.

"It's . . . a . . . Go back to bed, Diana." He lowered his voice. "Ella, for heaven's sake! Fun's fun, but . . . What do you want?"

"A drinkie."

"No! Certainly not! You're not coming in. I don't care if it is your damned Scots New Year. Do you hear? You're not coming in! And for God's sake leave us alone!"

"Oh," said his new wife behind him.

11

I had seen her coming. So, I'm sure, had Ella. Diana had taken out her curlers in a frenzy of activity there on the landing, but her black hair still showed the marks of them. She had the kind of face which, without it, cries plaintively for makeup.

I had never met Diana. And I had forgotten, if I'd been told, that Eric was now in Hong Kong, though it was natural enough that he should be, with the only other alternatives Aden, the Seychelles, Fiji, or British Honduras, and one of them shaky. I felt sorry for Diana, then, even if she was looking straight at Ella with the concentrated loathing of someone who has spent her married life as a replacement for continuous high drama.

"Eric," Diana said. "Shut the door!"

"Yes . . . by Jove, I will!"

Ella put out her foot. She took a size seven even without the points.

"Why must you be like this?" she shouted. "I've asked you to dinner. I've asked you to parties. . . ."

"All we want is to be left alone!" Diana shouted back. "Eric, shut that door!"

"I can't very well. Look, Ella, be reasonable. If you want to talk . . . I mean, if there's any help you need . . . I'm perfectly willing to meet somewhere and . . ."

"No!" Diana said.

"My dear." Eric turned. "Please go back to bed. I'll handle things." He glared at me. "I'm astonished at you, Harris. Being party to something like this."

"Paul's staying with me."

"That doesn't surprise me, Ella. Practically nothing concerning you could surprise me."

"Then you shouldn't be so damn stuffy now."

"Blast it! One thirty in the morning! And I'm not feeling social! Quite aside from the whole thing being totally . . . inappropriate."

It was a good word to have found in that moment. I couldn't have done it.

"Come on, Ella," I said.

"Oh . . ."

I pulled her toward those concrete steps. The door slammed behind us. Ella went down sideways, with a childlike caution. I had every reason to feel angry for my unwitting part in this performance, but most of me wanted to laugh.

"I'd say it was only sporting, Ella, when you've divorced a man to leave him be."

"But I loved him! And I still do in a way. Besides, she doesn't give him enough to eat."

"What?"

She stood looking down at me.

"It's perfectly true. Eric's silly about food. You have to coax him. And she doesn't. I *know* she doesn't. He was always skinny but he's worse now. You know something? I think he misses me."

Ella had leaped up those steps all right, but she appeared to need help now. I put out a hand.

"Have you been seeing Eric?"

"Of course."

"Without his wife knowing?"

"Well, I didn't say he wasn't to tell her. We meet for lunch sometimes. He won't come to the house. One of his superiors might get to hear of that. Prominent public servant up to no good with his former wife. We meet in a restaurant downtown. A Chinese one that does a rather nice line in ham and eggs for Eric. He always liked ham and eggs."

She was crying.

"Come on, you silly woman," I said.

"But I only want to be friends, honestly. I'd be friends with Diana."

That called for no comment. I pulled her through the gate

13

and across the road. She was still crying when I drove the mini off.

I never want to live in a house over which a contemporary architect has been allowed a totally free hand. Ella's place was on the south shore of the island, stuck on a point which had previously, and sensibly, been left to a tumble of rocks and scrub pine. You went down to it from the high road, a roller-coaster drop of smooth concrete to a platform in front of the garages. It wasn't a very wide platform, and a careless miscalculation in the approach could put you in the swimming pool. It was a many-leveled house, chunks of shining new concrete pasted onto native stone, and inside you couldn't look too closely at the decor without the risk of falling down a lethal flight of four shallow steps. No expense had been spared to give you the feeling you had been asked to stay in the reception area of a very modern cinema designed to exhibit sexy art films. I don't think Yamabushi, the architect, could ever have met Ella; or if he had, it was malice which made him decide to do the vast living room in sunrise pink. He was his own decorator, probably because no one else could be found to carry on where he left off.

The room was full of interest. One wall was entirely devoted to a mural by Bundonji, who recently had a retrospective exhibition in New York to which I was taken, and I remember a warning by the artist himself in the catalogue: "Painting must never speak, it must never indicate, it must never cry out." This mural just moaned, all eighteen feet of it, a magenta and green noise.

When that room first burst on me Ella had watched my face.

"Well, I was brought up with Scots mahogany," she said.

One window wall curved out and was followed by a vast sofa covered in what looked like polar bear skin. You walked on multicolored mosaic tiling until you fell onto the central carpet, two inches thick and roughly ten yards in diameter. On this was a minimum of furniture suffering from a Japanese influence and built to give you disc trouble. *The International Architect* had featured the house with fourteen illustrations in an article called "Yamabushi in Hong Kong." It certainly wasn't Ella in Hong Kong. In it she suggested a displaced character actress whimpering for a producer.

"Put on a record," Ella said from the curved sofa where she was sitting on ocelot to protect herself from white bear.

I put on Lise Berens singing "Happen That Man." Lise's sound comes out like something pulled over vocal cords sprinkled with broken bottles, but it's all punch.

"How did you know I'd like that so much?" Ella asked. "How did you know?"

I poured whisky into mauve Yugoslav glass, hating to do it. Ella looked at me over the edge of her beaker.

"Well, you do worry about someone you were married to for years. You *do*. Besides, Eric needs looking after."

"And Diana's not doing it?"

Ella shook her head.

"You just don't understand. It's terribly hard for Eric these days. He has to live on his salary. He has no money of his own, and he grew used to mine."

"What about his wife's Post Office savings?"

"She hasn't a penny. He met her on the rebound from me, just after I'd married Miguel. In London. She was a journalist, of all things. On one of those weeklies that tell you to read the books you damn well won't. Diana is starving in Hong Kong, Eric says. Intellectually. It worries him. He was worried tonight."

"I noticed."

"It's why he yapped at us. He had to, with Diana breathing on his neck. He wanted to have us in, really."

"I wouldn't have said so."

"I *know* how Eric feels." Her mouth drooped.

"Ella, please don't cry into that whisky. I brought it to you, remember? And it's too good to be salted. If you're so worried about Eric why don't you make a settlement on him?"

"But I tried to! When we bust up. It seemed only fair. Why should women always get the alimony? He wouldn't hear of it. And he won't now."

I stared.

"You offered him money down there in your Chinese restaurant?"

"Yes. He was shocked. You'd think I had said that Britannia didn't rule the waves any more. Something that hit him on the raw. And then I said would you mind if I left you some in my will and he said that inherited money is different. Though why the hell it should be I can't see. After all, it isn't as if people aren't gobbling more and more Bain's biscuits every year. And he knows that."

"Did Miguel take a settlement?"

"He snapped it up and wanted more. I gave him twenty thousand pounds. I thought ten thousand a year for two years was enough to pay for my Latin experiment. And that was quite different, of course. I didn't really feel married to Miguel, ever. It wouldn't have surprised me to learn he was a bigamist."

"Quite likely he was."

"You think me an utter fool, don't you? About people? About men?"

I moved over, put her glass on a table, sat down on ocelot and kissed Ella.

"Pet," she said.

"That's one thing I'm not."

Kirsty coughed from a far corner of the room where she could have been standing for some time. Ella sat up and patted her hair.

"Oh, hello, darling. Happy New Year."

"The same to you and many of them, Miss Ella."

Then Kirsty looked at me. I had never assessed my rating in that quarter and had the feeling now of being an intruder on small domestic detail.

"Have a drinkie, dear? Break down just for once?"

"You know I'm temperance, Miss Ella. Everything's ready."

"Of course, darling. I'll be right along."

Kirsty left us. Ella kept her voice down.

"Paul, it's potty, but we have a little party every New Year. Sometimes I've nearly had to crawl to it, but I've always got there. And Kirsty always sits up waiting. It only lasts twenty minutes. But I have to eat haggis."

"In Hong Kong?"

"Yes. Kirsty has it flown out from Brechin. Pour me an enormous whisky to wash down the stuff, will you? She takes hers with orange squash. It's really the weirdest tradition, but I have to go through with it. For just a moment I thought she was going to ask you, too, but . . ."

"You go on."

Ella was lucky to have Kirsty. Her status was undefined. She wasn't a maid and she wasn't a housekeeper, but one of that almost extinct species of family retainer who attach themselves and stay in orbit for no very obvious reason. If Ella had had children Kirsty would have supervised the Chinese amahs, keeping a vigilant eye on the rearing of young Bains to see that they didn't come under too strong Oriental influences. Kirsty had stayed with Ella through two marriages and the gap between them. She wore, summer and winter, dresses run up by herself, usually gray, though sometimes dark blue. She had jet beads for gala occasions and a permanently cold eye for the world around Ella, which included me. The fact of my Scots blood helped a little, but it was a poor kind of Scotsman who could afford to live well in his own land and didn't. For the Far East Kirsty retained a reserved distrust. Ella was daft not to be living in her good stone house near Dundee, but if this was the kind of life she liked . . . well.

I had never been able to hold Kirsty in talk for long. She was civil, but with a hint of strain, and she slid around our contacts with an eel-like dexterity, getting clear and away quickly. You never knew in that house, or in any of Ella's houses, where you would meet Kirsty. She materialized, on mysterious and uncharted missions, always with a good Presbyterian air of being busy. Busyness was an end in living. You filled your days with it and went to bed at night with a kind of shame for this permitted sloth. A cold bed, too, Ella had told me. Kirsty would have nothing to do with this caper of electric blankets and the like, and wherever Yamabushi had put her room it had the heat turned off and all the windows open.

I could have done with a Kirsty in the places I lived in, to help fill up an emptiness that is somehow never eased by the breathing of servants. My rooms seem always to be big, and when I move them the ghosts come with me.

The phone rang when I was lying along the sofa with my eyes shut. The wall clock was a gilt hand moving round the signs of the Zodiac and a rough estimate, which was the best you could do from that thing, put time at about two fifteen.

"Paul Harris here."

I heard an indrawn breath. Then the receiver at the other end went down with a click.

When Ella came back she said, "Wasn't that the telephone?"

"Yes. Mystery caller. Hung up on my gruff voice."

"But how odd!" Ella said that on a note that was remarkably false for her. "Man or woman?"

"Hard to tell from just breathing."

She looked at me, with those remarkable eyes very wide.

"Paul, what are you thinking?"

"That one of the troubles about life in Hong Kong is the way people keep on making wrong-number calls in the small hours of the morning."

When Ella laughed she relaxed into it. Her shoulders were still shaking as she turned away to add more whisky to the haggis.

In my own room I didn't sleep for a long time. I wasn't

exactly pushed off to bed, but there was that feeling around that my hostess thought the day spent and wanted to wrap it up. When I said I was sleepy she claimed to be just dropping herself, though her eyes appeared to me to have a remarkably bright glitter still.

It was a good bed, not overly soft, and the window beside it was low to let you see out from your pillow on a moonlit night. The moon had gone, leaving only the grumble of the sea down there in an inky blackness.

There was a sound like a vampire bat trying to break down the glass, then a scrabbling on a high ledge, then a plop on the floor. Ella's ridiculously named Siamese cat, apparently displaced, screeched at me.

"You've got the wrong window, Heather."

Heather didn't think so. She got up on my bed making a noise like a hydroelectric dynamo switched on. Through this row I just heard the popping of a motor scooter up on the highway. Then that cut out, and there was only Heather, telling me she liked me.

2

The cat had gone for breakfast when I woke. I sat up and looked at the sea. It was right down there, expensive jade this morning, a translucent glowing out to a line of still lasting gray mist. One of the attendant British islands pulled itself up out of shining water, making a little hump of its own importance. There were seven junks in a row, square-sailed and highly relevant to this setting, but apparently without purpose, held on a polished surface where there was no wind. A pine thrust out spiked arms below and above my window, framing what I saw with an elaborately designed naturalness. The Japanese can always make a pine do what they want, and probably Yamabushi had imported this one from under Mount Fuji, all wrapped up in straw and at a cost to Ella of two thousand dollars.

Trust a Japanese, too, to find the one site on a packed island from which you couldn't look out of any window and see signs of ordinary human living. Maybe Ella had wanted a house near death, but what she had got was as isolated from any rough unpleasantness as a Zen monastery. Out on these rocks was a bought silence, with the sea beyond like a scroll painting designed for contemplative repose while you sat propped up on an inner-spring mattress. It was my sea down there, with the names along it the landmarks of my life, Haiphong, Palawan,

Singora, Kra, wonderful bells of sound, but places where the living isn't always pretty and hasn't been for me.

There was a knock on the door. It was Tang, a Hailam houseboy, an exile now, but not apparently troubled by this. He had the unnervingly unmarked face of so many Chinese, smooth and taut, thin flesh on hard bone. He could have been twenty-five or fifty, moving like neither, in a kind of deliberate gracefulness he had evolved for himself.

"Breakfast," he said, flattering me with Cantonese and a smile.

"Have you taken in Miss Bain's tray yet?"

"No. Too soon for waking, maybe."

"Then bring it here when it's ready."

Ella was Miss Bain in her house, like an actress with her own identity immune to husbands.

I had my breakfast by the window and was finished before Tang brought the second tray. I took this along to Ella's door and opened that onto curtained darkness, finding a table and then moving over to windows, groping for a cord. The curtains probably operated electronically, but I couldn't find any switch and had to yank at them.

Daylight came in. The room was too hot, and I opened a door onto a balcony.

"Ella! Wakey!"

Her bed was seven feet wide and recessed into a wall, at night indirectly illumined like a stage set. A great mound of pillows were heaped up to the feet of a bored-looking stork woven into silk. Ella had bouts of asthma when she needed to prop herself up, and the pillows were for that. Now she was lost in them, and rather lost in that vast bed, too, just a neat ridge down the middle. The covers were pulled up to her neck and all I saw was her ginger hair, tousled.

"It'll soon be eleven."

She didn't move. I had the tray again, half kneeling against the bed, and I put the tray down on the covers, reaching out

21

with one hand for her shoulder. There was no stirring of her body under my hand at all. I had to get right onto the bed to lift and turn her, and her face, when I saw it, had a stunned look, the eyes closed. Then her jaw went slack and her mouth opened.

It wasn't Ella at all; it was that stranger, death.

I knew this even before I fumbled under the covers for her arm and her wrist. Her body was still warm, but she had no pulse.

I couldn't stand that sagging jaw. I picked up a traveling clock, snapped it shut, and pushed it under her chin. Then, still looking at her, my hand went out for the phone. Dialing seemed to take a long time.

All right, it's a cliché that we partly die with those we love, but we do. And in those seconds I could hear doors slamming that would never be opened again for me or anyone. Big, blundering Scots girl who took a kind of fire where she walked, along with the whisky. Her laugh was from a throat scraped by too many cigarettes all the time, and too many glasses reached for over too many years. I stood by her bed dialing, thinking what I hadn't done for Ella when I could have, all those things, the long list of them from which I had turned with the laugh of a man who isn't pinning himself on anything. Eric, Miguel, and Ella with her arms round my neck saying, "Marry me. We would make it work, we would." And then that withdrawal again, as though she had caught sight of how she looked in some invisible mirror, with her flowing un-disciplined body in which she could never quite believe as some man's sole comfort. "In the morning I'm hell, darling." That's what I'd expected with her tray, the voice from the pillows, angry at curtains drawn away from the hard, white, living light. She couldn't fear the living light again.

Her eyes were closed. I've seen many dead with eyes wide, frozen lenses of a last fear. But Ella's were closed, as by a gentle hand.

22

"Hello, hello? Could I speak to Dr. MacAndrew, please?"

"This is Louise."

"Oh. Paul, here. . . ."

"I know."

"Louise, I must speak to Archie!"

"He's gone to his surgery downtown. Over an hour ago. Is anything wrong?"

"I can't talk about it. Could you give me his number down there?"

"Is anything wrong with Ella?"

"Look, Louise, please just give me that number!"

"It's Tai Shan three-nine-four-six. So it *is* Ella?"

I clipped down the receiver, lifted it, and dialed again. The receptionist had a smile in her voice. She wanted to help me.

"Dr. MacAndrew. At once. It's urgent."

"I'm afraid he's just left for his clinic in Kowloon. Is it an emergency?"

"Yes."

"Then I'll put you through to his partner, Dr. MacGregor."

I didn't know MacGregor, he certainly hadn't been at the party, but his voice was Scots, an overfed and hot-sounding voice, but efficient, painstakingly efficient. He asked me three medical questions, and the last one made me look at Ella again. Her lips were blue, almost black, and I told him.

"Aye. Well, I'll be right round."

"Do you think a heart attack?"

"Could be . . . yes. Does anyone else in the house know about this?"

"Not yet."

"It's a good idea in cases like this to leave things the way they were. You moved the body?"

"I lifted her . . . yes."

"Pity. Just leave everything now, turn the key in the door, and keep it for me."

He hung up. I looked at the bed with the feeling that there

ought to be something I could do, something useful and sensible. There wasn't. All I did was carry the tray over to a table again, then go to the windows and, after closing the balcony door, pull the curtains a little.

I was putting the key in the outside lock when I looked up to see Kirsty with her hands folded.

"Why are you doing that? What's up with Miss Ella?"

It took me a moment to answer, under those almost black eyes.

"She's had a heart attack. She's dead."

The sound Kirsty made was in her throat. She didn't open her mouth at all. She went past me, and I didn't try to keep her out of the bedroom. She walked quite slowly over to the bed and stood there, still with her hands in front of her, looking down at what was in it. She didn't make any move to touch the body lying in deep softness.

I thought then that some women have children on whom they can have no real claim, either from mind or body. Kirsty was now old and barren and she had been neither until this moment. She was still erect, but her face grew shriveled and puckered, as thought her own living was burning out behind a mask. Her lips moved, but I couldn't hear any words.

She turned her head to me quite suddenly. "Have you got the police, then?" The strength in her voice was startling.

"No. The doctor's on his way."

She began to walk back toward me. The burning fire was in her eyes.

"It's the police we'll be wanting."

She went by.

"Kirsty!"

She didn't turn; she was going away from me, to a corner in a passage, to lose herself in the carefully designed labyrinths of this house.

I couldn't just go after her; there was a key to be turned, and when that was done I didn't follow an old woman to whatever sanctuary she had. I went instead to the sitting room, which was tidy and empty, ready for the day. From somewhere in the house came the hum of a vacuum cleaner, a sound of busyness. No one had stopped a routine busyness as yet. Then the cleaner cut out, and the sound of the sea came through an open window.

I went out onto a terrace cluttered with potted plants put there by gardeners who had to have something to do, being Chinese. I stared south, wishing I hadn't been here on this morning. It was something to learn about from a long way off, when you had routine to reach for as a cover.

A sampan passed under the point of rocks beneath, one man in it, trawling lines behind him for fish. He began to sing one of those songs that sound too old to have any personal reference to the singer at all, just a tune carried neatly over the centuries on the thin, neutral voices of the singers. He didn't look at the lines out behind as he moved back and forth on the stern oar, leaving the fish to hook themselves on or not. He was a man in blue in a new white deal boat with lifted prow, rocking himself over a glistening bay.

Dr. MacGregor came into Ella's sitting room with the air of someone who never notices his surroundings. He was broad-shouldered, with a head hunched down on them, and looked as though he went through life with few beliefs to encumber him, but with great determination. He was hairy, and even in the suiting which a Hong Kong winter permitted, this made him just slightly sinister. His wrists stuck out from his cuffs, and the black fur on them came down onto the fingers of big, capable hands.

Dr. MacGregor sat down at once in the manner of a man who expects to have his lead followed. He didn't appear to mind the long descent into that low chair, though he did dislike having to peer up at me.

"Asphyxia," he said.

"What?"

"That's what she died of. Asphyxia. Suffocation."

"You mean it wasn't her heart?"

"Not directly. Clear signs of suffocation."

"But . . . how can you suffocate in bed?"

"Not easy. There have been cases. Quite common with children in slums. Overlaying."

"Are you telling me that Ella suffocated in her pillows?"

"So it would appear at the moment. There are no indications of a coronary. Did she go to bed drunk?"

"No."

"You're sure? It's New Year. Miss Bain didn't have much of a reputation for moderation."

"She was not drunk when she went to bed."

"You know because you were with her, Mr. Harris?"

"I was not with Ella in her room."

He made no comment on that. Instead, he pushed himself up from the chair and went over to the telephone.

"You haven't called the police, Mr. Harris?"

"No, I was waiting for you."

He nodded and picked up the receiver. He jiggled the hooks. "This line is dead."

"Then it hasn't been switched over."

He watched me go to a little box beyond an arch.

"What are you doing?"

"Connecting you up. Ella liked a private phone to her bed. This switch cuts off the other house phones. Puts everything straight through to her."

"Seems an odd arrangement."

"It's quite ordinary if you conduct business from your house as Ella did and want to be sure of privacy."

MacGregor looked at me as though assessing my apparent calm. Then he began to dial, carefully, with a hairy forefinger.

"Dr. Robert MacGregor here. Get me Inspector Mitchell, please."

He glanced over his shoulder to suggest that he would prefer to be alone. I went through the open glass door to the terrace and closed it behind me. There was the rumble of his voice, but no words.

How quickly we can establish the dead as such in our minds, reaching out for a cord that pulls down a blind. MacGregor had helped me to do this. A doctor comes out from his mysterious movements in a room of death, and all that is left behind is a body, nothing to weep over. You weep for something else, most often yourself, if you do at all.

Tang was below me, on one of the steep paths, talking to a man with a twig broom. Tang was using his hands. It was a moment of intense, dramatic mime, the squeaking of voices not relevant. The houseboy had got the word, all right. He looked back at the house, saw me, and his hands fluttered still. The hired man pushed the broom back into movement again, back at his work of polishing up that non-garden. Tang began to climb the path toward me, his walk a kind of fluid innocence, and he didn't acknowledge me there by a second look, going without any haste down steps to the swimming pool and then out of sight.

I looked up at the balcony outside Ella's windows. The whole façade of the house was irregular, with projections and withdrawals, but that balcony struck an odd note of afterthought, as though it was something Ella had insisted on, probably against protest. It had a staircase, too, spiral concrete which had let Ella go straight to the pool from her room. It would also let anyone in the garden go straight up to Ella's room without anyone in the house being any the wiser.

I couldn't see her made nervous by the thought of a prowler able to stand just outside the room in which she was sleeping. Ella had never shared that frequent uneasiness of the rich for their persons and their possessions. In Singapore she had slept on an unscreened upstairs veranda right through a time of anti-European riots because she found the air-conditioned room behind it stuffy. I thought of the heat in her bedroom when I went in. Ella loved heat, but not to sleep in. At night she would open a window, like any other good Scot. It would have been done before she climbed into that great bed.

The whisky might have killed Ella, quite suddenly, but it hadn't. I knew that then, with all the gleaming conviction of an old spaewife.

MacGregor came out onto the terrace.

"The police are on the way. They're bringing their own surgeon, but I'm waiting."

"Dr. MacGregor, do I take it that you would not sign a certificate giving asphyxia as a natural cause of death?"

His blue eyes were on me for a minute. "I would not."

"Does this mean an autopsy?"

"It depends on the police surgeon, Mr. Harris. But I'd say yes."

"And an inquest?"

"Probably. Damn lot of nonsense, that."

"Why?"

"Because a coroner's jury is a collection of idiots passing a verdict on something they're incapable of assessing scientifically. We do the job a damn sight better in Scotland with the Fiscal and the police between them. But it's English law here, more's the pity."

"Is it your opinion that Ella may have been murdered?"

I had the perhaps curious feeling then that he warmed to me, just a little.

"Such an opinion is outside my province, Mr. Harris. Also, Miss Bain was not my patient. Asphyxia has not been confirmed."

"But you were sure a few minutes ago."

"I still am. But we can't be definite until the autopsy."

"That should make the cause of death clear?"

"Quite clear. What are you driving at?"

"My own position, Dr. MacGregor. It's tricky."

"You mean . . . because you are living in the house?"

"No. But unless Ella has changed it I'm a major beneficiary under her will. I forget the exact sum. But it was somewhere in the region of a quarter of a million pounds."

MacGregor clearly didn't startle easily. But now surprise seemed to make him swell, at the same time sinking that head deeper into muscular shoulders. The whole effect was almost simian; that is, if you could imagine a neatly suited ape with the highest professional qualifications and a Scots burr.

"My God!" he said.

Inspector Mitchell was a Scotsman, too. I had expected this. It seemed inevitable on New Year's day in Hong Kong. He was tall, lean, and more than slightly melancholic, with a Glasgow inflection rising to a sharp lightness at the end of each sentence which made him seem to be asking questions even when he wasn't. He kept looking at me out of gentle brown eyes in which I didn't believe for one moment, as though he was really a family man who had somehow landed in the wrong calling. He had big feet and this troubled him. He kept pushing them about and finally curled them under an upright chair in Ella's workroom in a manner that was almost coy. He also chain smoked and went into paroxysms of controlled coughing which should have put him at a disadvantage, but somehow didn't.

I was sitting behind Ella's desk, a piece of deliberate strategy on my part. In almost any interview between two people one dominates the other. I was fighting to serve the surprises rather than receive them. Beyond a closed door were sounds, for Ella's bedroom was almost opposite and they were taking her body away from the house she had built to be near death in life. I half wondered what she had meant by that, and didn't know, in the way we don't know what friends mean by words thrown out. If there had been in the disorderly sprawl of her personality a streak of the religious, this hadn't been advertised to me. Not at any time.

'How long have you known about this will, Mr. Harris?"

"Five years."

"A long time. You don't think she made a new one?"

"She may have. But I hardly think so. Not without telling me."

"Have I got this straight . . . there was no suggestion that you were to act as trustee of the money?"

"Not in the will. It was left to me outright. As I remember the wording I could, if I wanted, use the money for my own purposes."

"And you have just told me that you are now in Hong Kong to raise money?"

"Yes."

He coughed and then suppressed a spasm.

"You don't have to answer this . . . but are you in any financial difficulties, Mr. Harris?"

"I don't mind answering at all. I'm not. I wanted the money for a specific business purpose. To finance a new enterprise."

"And what sort of sum were you hoping to raise in Hong Kong?"

I looked into those brown eyes.

"A quarter of a million would serve me very nicely indeed."

Mitchell pulled another cigarette from his case. He didn't offer me one because I had a cigar going, a good aromatic Manila. He took a little time getting his light. It was a cheap lighter.

"Can you tell me something about this legacy to . . . a friend?"

"Certainly. And you can confirm what I tell you with my lawyer in Singapore. He's Russell Menzies, of Menzies and Harland. He drew up the will. And he knows all the circumstances."

30

Mitchell wrote down the name and address in his little book. The house was quiet beyond us. An engine started up outside it, an ambulance going away. I had then a stab of feeling which didn't serve this moment, the thought of Ella in this damn architectural masterpiece for which she held the title deeds. And which held her clothes. Why had the fool come to Hong Kong?

The phone rang on the desk. The inspector moved very quickly, but I got the receiver.

"Paul Harris here."

A man coughed.

"Ah . . . Mr. Harris, I'm Winton Peebles, Miss Bain's solicitor here. The police have just told me . . . the terrible news."

"Yes."

"I was wondering if there is anything I can do at this stage. And then, of course, you're an executor with me. Perhaps we ought to meet."

"Why don't you come here?"

"To the house?"

"Yes. I think the police are about finished."

"The police? Oh, of course, sudden death. Yes. Quite. Very well, what time?"

"In about an hour."

Mitchell had pushed his feet out in front of him again and was looking at them. I hung up.

"That was Miss Bain's solicitor here, Inspector. It appears I'm still executor. That means the will hasn't been changed."

"I see. You were telling me about it?"

"Yes. The background is simply that Ella was faced with one of the problems of the rich: how to leave their money well. Except for her brother she had no close relations, so there were no family obligations. I seem to remember small legacies, and there may have been codicils since. I think I know of one."

"Who?"

"Her ex-husband. They remained friends."

"A generous woman, Mr. Harris."

"Very."

"And your role in this? You had verbal instructions what you were to do with your legacy?"

"Yes. We discussed things in considerable detail, a project to use this money. I may say it's one that appeals to me, too. In fact, I suggested it. I'm to build with Ella's money an orphanage for Chinese kids in Singapore. It's to be put in Johore somewhere, right away from the mess of the city that spawned them."

He looked at me.

"Have you any idea why Miss Bain didn't plan a trust for this?"

"There are two reasons. Firstly, a quarter of a million will provide buildings and start the thing off. But it won't endow it properly. That was my end, to build up the endowment, if I survived her. Ella thought I would for some reason. Secondly, she didn't much like trusts. Her father left one in which she got no authority in the business at all until she was thirty. It was very shortsighted of the old man. Ella was a natural business woman, as she showed in a few years. When she could, she practically paralyzed a Dundee board of directors by moving in and doing things. I'd hazard that Bain's Bakeries came near to doubling their profits under her hand. But she was helpless until she was too old to make it a life. She had other habits by then. One of them was whisky, another living in the East. Am I making the situation plain?"

"It's not a very plain situation."

"It seems so to me."

"Perhaps that's because you're in a position to understand the conscience of the rich," he said, showing that he had read the latter-day classics. Or looked at them.

"Inspector, the trust I accepted from Ella wasn't a legal one. It is nonetheless a trust."

32

"Again you don't have to answer me . . . but if you get this money will you use it all for the orphanage in Malaya?"

"Yes."

"In your own good time, perhaps?"

"In my own good time."

"Which could mean a temporary investment of that money in some enterprise, perhaps to increase its value?"

"No. I shan't play with Ella's money."

Mitchell took out his notebook again. It was small enough to have been a gentleman's diary. He turned over a couple of pages, looking at his notes.

"I'd like to go over one or two points, Mr. Harris. You went with Miss Bain to her bedroom door, and you say this was about half past two in the morning?"

"Round about."

"You stood by an open door? You saw into the room?"

"Up to a point, I suppose."

"And everything you could see looked perfectly normal?"

"Yes. What are you getting at? That the murderer was in there waiting?"

"No one has said anything about a murderer as yet, Mr. Harris."

"Then isn't it about time we started?"

"Why?"

"I like the facts laid out in front of me before I start assessing them."

"And you're called on to assess these facts?"

"For my own sake, yes, Inspector. You're not forgetting that phone call I told you about? The one that came just before we went to bed."

He looked at his hands, flexing the fingers as though to test them against an arthritic threat he kept secret.

"I don't feel that the phone call is of much use to us at the moment, Mr. Harris. No voice, no clue from that."

"There's the fact that it happened."

He looked at me.

"Yes."

Then he stood.

"Thank you for your candor."

His tone suggested that any outstanding display of candor was something which immediately rang bells in the police mind. We went together into the hall, and he paused by Ella's door, his hand on the knob.

"I'd prefer it, Mr. Harris, if you were available in this house today."

"I won't leave the grounds."

That earned me a nod. The door shut him away.

I walked down a corridor. Even the police and an after-death bustle hadn't given this house any feel of mourning at all. Ella was gone, but you weren't confronted with reminders of her, any more than you would have been in a hotel suite. Send off the clothes and the shoes and clear the dressing table; change the flowers and open up for business again. The rich tend to live in this kind of place these days, the decor restfully impersonal. Put a pot of your own out anywhere and it screams against the designer's intent.

Someone else had been walking down another corridor from the front door. We met at right angles to each other in the pink room. I took a deep breath and held it for a second.

The girl looking at me had the kind of thick, heavy, slightly coarse Chinese hair that doesn't get a good market price from the wigmakers but is just fine on the grower's head. She wore it very long indeed, in defiance of any fashion that wasn't her line, right to the shoulders, the movement of that hair part of head movement, and calculated. She was thin, but tallish, with the kind of bones which give you the feeling they'll snap under any big rough pressure. Her hands were very small indeed, and so were her feet. Her eyes weren't; authentic sloping almonds all right, but they could be made to go wide. They were wide now as she looked at me.

34

"I'm Lia Fan. I phoned Ella a little while ago and got Tang instead. I came here in a taxi, needing a double brandy all the way. Are you going to give it to me?"

Her voice suggested Beverly Hills High School, or an American employer sometime early, or just a lot of visits to the pictures. She was not beautiful, with too much mouth and too pale a skin, with no light under it, but very few men would have paused to consider this kind of detail. The general effect was the kind of secretary I'm always advertising for and never get.

What she said about telephoning was interesting, particularly in view of the fact that I'd been very alert for calls to the house after I found Ella. And the only time Miss Fan could have rung and got Tang instead of me was exactly twenty minutes when I was in Ella's bedroom with the police. And that was all of an hour and a half ago. It had been a long taxi ride from where this girl lived.

At the drinks cabinet I was thoughtful. Somehow Lia Fan wasn't quite the type I'd have expected Ella to have around as a close associate. Ella had never chosen to decorate her home with women better looking than herself. She had been forced to have them to parties sometimes, but that was as far as it went. And even allowing for Lia Fan working mornings only, which I knew, men sometimes turn up in the morning, too. It was odd. From the little Ella had said about her secretary I'd expected a mouse. This was no mouse.

Oriental women—and even the totally emancipated ones never quite lose it—have a very pretty trick of appearing to spend large portions of their lives just waiting for a clear male lead in a bewildering world. When I turned with the drinks there was Lia Fan waiting like that, doing a positive mime of lesser sex expecting light from natural lord in trousers. It wasn't in any way overplayed, she didn't take her brandy glass in both hands and raise it to forehead in obeisance, but for all that I had been appointed O. C. of the situation.

35

She drank her brandy. Miss Fan was not unused to alcohol. But when she spoke I still got a slight jolt again from her voice, from that hint of granite chips in it.

"Thanks. I really needed that. Have the police all gone?"

"No. The inspector's about still. Didn't you see his car outside?"

Her answer was immediate.

"I saw a car. I didn't look at it. Is it true . . . what Tang said about Ella?"

"What did Tang say?"

"That . . . they suspect she was killed."

"Yes. It's true."

Her eyes were wide again.

"Do you mind if I sit down? My knees feel weak."

Nice knees they were, too, displayed from a chair. She had thin legs, but not skinny, the kind of legs you see on a horse that can go fast. Those legs would still be good looking when Lia Fan was a granny.

"I believe you came here four days a week, Miss Fan?"

"Yes. Sometimes five if there was a lot of work. Not often. There wasn't a lot of work, really. Even for an inefficient secretary."

"Are you inefficient?"

"As a secretary, yes. My typing is poor, my shorthand worse."

That's what I'd always found with the ones who looked like this, together with the most elementary filing system as something totally beyond their comprehension. But none of the lovelies had been capable of such an honest assessment of their own professional worth.

"Would you mind answering one or two questions?" I asked.

"Of course I will."

She didn't suggest that her answers couldn't be important.

"Was Ella drinking in the mornings recently?"

36

Eyes went wide again.

"You must have known her very well. To ask that."

"Had she been?"

"Yes."

"For how long?"

"About two weeks. But why . . . ?"

"Miss Fan, Ella was very nearly an alcoholic. You probably wouldn't see it. She had certain rules she kept to . . . most of the time. One of them was nothing to drink before one. That was the way she kept balance. And it worked, too, for her. She wasn't over the edge. But she was pretty near it. And once or twice she's toppled. It happened in Singapore, when she broke up with her first husband. I had to gather up something at the bottom of a pretty steep slope."

"What . . . did you do?"

"I put her in a nerve clinic for well-heeled boozers, both Chinese and European. Charming place, on an island. If you try to swim for it the sharks get you. There have been some remarkable cures effected out there. Ella came back in two months."

"She was cured?"

"She was back to drinking nothing before one o'clock. On the rules again. You can see what I'm getting at. If the rules were thrown overboard recently she had something on her mind. Very much on it. Two weeks ago, you said."

"That was when I first noticed."

"How bad was it?"

"I took in her letters. She liked to do them in bed. That morning she just couldn't speak. Later she said it was a hangover. But it wasn't."

"And how often in the two weeks?"

"Well, of course, I was looking for it. But I'd say most mornings. Then three days ago, just before you came, she said she had fallen out of bed. She wouldn't allow the curtains to be drawn. I wanted to call the doctor, but she shouted at me.

She told me to go home, that the letters could wait. I went to the study and about an hour later Tang came in and said I was to go home. I haven't been here since."

This girl had shown no grief for Ella. Talk of murder had made her weak at the knees, but there had been no sign of tears. As a member of the employing classes I flatter myself that I have a real personal relationship with the people in my office. I like to picture them going around that first day white-faced at the shock of my loss. Maybe they wouldn't. But I'd still like them to be less cool than Miss Fan. It was just possible, of course, that the double brandy had restored her. And perhaps it's not easy for a girl to weep for the loss of a woman boss, particularly a woman like Ella, who had great impatience with her own sex which carried over easily into outright animosity. I couldn't recall a close woman friend of Ella's. For her, women were a waste of man-hours.

Lia Fan was suddenly staring at something beyond me, sitting bolt upright in her chair to do it. I turned.

Louise MacAndrew was standing under the arch of that corridor to the front door. She could have been there for quite some time.

3

I thought then that for a house where a murder may have been committed this one was remarkably easy to get into. But Louise would brush policemen aside. She was standing now like someone who has been contemplating a deft, silent withdrawal.

"Oh, Paul!" she said.

Then she came toward us, or rather me. Lia Fan might not have been there at all. The Chinese girl stood; but that didn't get her noticed, though there was a tension between the two women that even I could feel, tightening as Louise closed in.

Lia snapped that tension.

"I'll be in the study," she said to me.

They passed on the carpet without even the smallest of greetings, no tiny charm-school nod.

"I hope you don't mind my coming like this," Louise said. "I finally got Archie. It's been a shock to him, too. And we both want you to come to us. Right now. Just pack your bags. I've got a car outside."

Lia had disappeared.

"The police wouldn't like it," I said.

"The police? I don't understand?"

"It's simple. I was staying here. Ella may have been murdered."

39

Those top-drawer English girls have a built-in immunity to shock. Perhaps nothing can seem very dreadful after eight years of wearing a school uniform which encases the growing female in a chrysalis of drab wool. The end product is usually a pretty conservative butterfly, too, pastel colored and trained only for restricted flights.

"Ella murdered?" Louise said in a tea-party tone. "I can't believe it."

And then, quite suddenly, at least half a dozen good reasons why a woman like Ella should have met this kind of end occurred to her. She stood there contemplating each one separately. It was quite some time before she said, "But how unpleasant for you."

"Yes."

Louise looked around her then.

"And in this lunatic house."

"Some Chinese will want to buy it. Prestige place. Can I get you a drink?"

"Oh, no. But I would like to go outside. This room . . . isn't very private."

We went out on the terrace. I moved an azalea brought to bloom under glass and sat on the balustrade. Louise chose an iron chair on which she sat without an inspection, assuming that someone would have wiped away any bird droppings even on a crisis morning.

"Who told you about Ella?" I asked. "MacGregor?"

She nodded.

"But he just said Ella was dead. I can scarcely believe— Paul, will the police keep the investigations quiet if they are looking for a . . . a murderer?"

"I shouldn't think so."

"You mean . . . the papers will get hold of this?"

"They probably have it now."

"That *is* horrible," Louise said.

She looked much less calm. The papers were something you

only got into via the social columns. Then I was positively startled.

"Did Lia Fan stay here last night, Paul?"

She was very familiar with the name of someone she hadn't noticed.

"Certainly not. Did she sometimes?"

"I wouldn't know. I just wondered."

"What do you know about Lia Fan?"

Louise pulled off her gloves. "Quite a lot. I discharged her for theft."

No wonder we'd come out here and shut the glass door carefully behind us. Louise looked at me.

"Oh, I didn't prosecute. Archie wouldn't let me. He said there were grounds for doubt. It was chivalrous of him. Because, of course, there weren't."

Something cold seemed to be sitting in my stomach.

"What did she steal?"

"Diamond earrings. Worth seven hundred pounds. She pawned them, too. The police got them back by a miracle. But she's a cool little piece. She didn't break down under questioning at all. And the middleman who bought them wouldn't identify her. They stick together."

She meant the Chinese stick together. It isn't really surprising in view of their general experience of the white races.

"And Ella just gave the girl a job?"

"Yes. I warned her. Not that I expected Ella to listen to me."

"Was Lia Fan your secretary?"

"Well, not really. Social secretary. It sounds a bit pompous. But one really has to have someone who will do that kind of thing out here. It's a very different world still from home."

"Which is why so many of us hang on through the riots," I said.

Louise chose to miss that. She stared thoughtfully out at a sea from which the haze had lifted. It was a hard blue out there, sun driving the winter-morning cold away.

41

"I'd like to know something about Lia Fan."

"Just what, Paul?"

"Who she is and where she comes from."

"I believe she was born in Nangking. But she was brought to relatives in Hong Kong as a child."

"Is she an orphan?"

"Maybe. I don't know. She went to a mission school here, or something like that. And then got jobs where she could."

"How did you get her?"

"From a friend who was going home."

"To whom Lia had given satisfaction?"

"Well, yes. She did give satisfaction in her job. I had no complaints there. In fact, I thought things were working out very well, until it happened."

"You sacked her. How long was it before she was working here?"

An iciness crept into Louise's voice.

"A matter of a few weeks."

"Louise, you're not suggesting that Ella took Lia Fan on to spite you in some way?"

"I don't think I like that question much, Paul. Why should Ella have any reason to want to spite me?"

"I'm wondering."

"Well, you can stop! We were social acquaintances, no more."

"Ella must have had some motive?"

"It's my experience that the Scots don't need a motive. They enjoy being bolshy."

It was a nice archaic word invented in British embassies just after World War I and brought home to the bright young things of the black-bottom era. Louise had probably caught it from her mama who, in her day, had almost certainly squeaked "Oh-de-oh-do" at Claridge's and been thrown into the Thames in a fringed evening dress from a houseboat. A little wild they had been then, but never bolshy. I couldn't resist the question.

"Do you find Archie bolshy?"

"Sometimes," Louise said.

I heard the phone ringing beyond glass and had to leave quickly. It went on ringing until I reached it, but before anything was said there was the tiny click of an extension cutting in. The house was full of extensions, and I could see Ella's point about that hall switch to cut them out.

It was Winton Peebles, the solicitor, again, and he sounded agitated.

"About coming up, Mr. Harris . . . I'm afraid it's not going to be too easy. You see, I've got Angus Bain here now."

"Have you?"

"He's in a very odd state, I'm afraid. In fact, I had to come away to my partner's office in order to ring you."

There was no way of shutting the fool up without letting the listener know I was aware of a presence on the line.

"Angus is bound to be upset," I said.

"It's a little more than that. He's really almost violent. And I'm afraid you're the cause. You see, he seems to feel that . . ."

"I can guess!"

"Oh. Can you?" I could practically hear Peebles groping about in his mind for the usual legal cautions. A sedative was called for, especially beamed toward our listener.

"Angus Bain and I have never seen eye to eye about anything, Mr. Peebles. I wouldn't worry about any noise he makes. He's been making a noise about something all his life, and to very little purpose. Get rid of him."

"I certainly want to. I think you should be told he knows he's not a legatee. And that you are."

I was surprised.

"How did he know that?"

"He says his sister told him."

I was even more surprised. But I got the man to leave things and hang up.

Louise was progressing across the pink room, with about

three quarters of the distance covered. She had her gloves on again and was looking thoughtful.

When Mitchell joined us from the corridor to the bedroom Louise showed no surprise. The inspector was carrying a lace-edged pillow from Ella's bed, very carefully, by one corner. He nodded, didn't mention the pillow, and went through the arch toward the front door. Louise would have been after him like a bullet if I hadn't said, gently, "Perhaps we'd better let the police get away before I see you to your car?"

She sent me a look which stated plainly that she rarely took any human relation to a depth from which a quick surfacing wasn't easy.

For a girl who had rated herself an inefficient secretary, Lia Fan was making a lot of noise on her typewriter. I knocked on the study door and opened it.

Lia had a portable on the main desk, with the telephone beside it. She was wearing black-rimmed glasses, which made her look like a Chinese lady novelist but not a romantic one. She was also too angry to pretend right now that she thought the other sex had all the brains.

"I'm busy, Mr. Harris. I thought I'd better get off letters to all the people I can think of who should know about Ella. I've a list here; would you like to check it?"

"No. Did you have a visit from the inspector?"

"I did. And I told him exactly what I told you. About Ella's recent drinking. I thought I'd better, since he might have been listening anyway. Also, a girl in my position should stick to one story. I'm sure Mrs. MacAndrew has put you completely in the picture about me?"

"She did her best," I said. "I came to see if you'd anything to add."

Lia Fan sat very still. She wasn't looking at me.

"Just one thing. Mrs. MacAndrew is a perfect lady. They're smooth liars when they want to be."

"You didn't steal any earrings?"

"I did not. It was one of the housemaids. And she knew that well enough."

"Why try to pin it on you?"

Lia Fan took off those spectacles. She dropped thick lashes, which were her own, and then lifted them again.

"It's awfully hard for a girl to put this delicately, Mr. Harris. But the doctor had started to notice me about the place, you might say. Not that he was really aware of this himself. But his wife got the message. Chinese gal full of guile. She make eyes at number-one Hong Kong medicine man. You savvy?"

"And did you make eyes at Archie?"

Lia Fan straightened in her chair.

"I like them younger and richer," she said gently.

She refused the cigarette I offered.

"Miss Fan, how did you get this job here?"

"There was an ad in the paper and I answered it. Any more questions?"

"One. The phone rang about twenty minutes ago. Why didn't you answer it?"

"It didn't seem likely to be for me this morning."

"Was the inspector with you when it rang?"

"No. He'd just gone."

I went away thinking that if Louise had imagined she could frame Lia Fan she was a fool.

It wasn't exactly swimming weather for Hong Kong, but Yamabushi had made Ella's an all-seasons pool. You went into a concrete cabaña and dialed the water temperature you wanted and then went out and smoked a cigar while the big bath heated up. By 3 P.M. I was lying on a rubber raft with my feet and arms in the water and a winter sun tickling my chest. A portable radio was beating out "I Got a Feelin'" by Harry Corwell and his Mud-Slingers, muted, but still beating it out. When I flicked drops of water at Heather she gave me a look from her Ben Turpin eyes and moved to a dry spot to lick furiously. None of this set a Scottish tone of mourning at all, and it was exactly what Ella would have wanted. Or so I thought.

Little white, separate clouds were coming straight from Red China but without any propaganda on them. I lay there thinking that I was still of an age for a setting like this to need a woman to round it out, and that made me think of Lia Fan, but I didn't get her; I got Archie MacAndrew. He came along the paving wearing no particular expression, not even a smile for my good sense. He sat down in a wicker chair and lit himself a cigarette. After a time, and when the radio was playing "You Spent It All," he said, "The poor bitch."

I nodded. He held smoke in his lungs in the way that is just asking for trouble.

"Sure you don't want to move in with us, Paul? I think I could fix it with the police."

"I'll stay here. Might have company."

"Who?"

"There's a lawyer downtown trying to restrain Angus Bain from violence. Toward me."

"That little runt."

"See much of him when you're over in Kowloon?"

"No. I don't go in for well-heeled saints."

"And yet it's a role you play yourself."

"Who said that?"

"Ella. Last night. Told me all about the good works. Fancy old Archie practicing at cut rates."

"No rates at all, you bastard."

"I wouldn't have believed it."

"Like to come over there with me?"

"No," I said.

Heather skirted a wet patch and jumped on Archie's knee. He looked at her.

"I don't like cats," he said.

"No Siamese is a cat. Make a lap for her."

He did. Heather circled once and settled.

"Paul, Ella got pretty drunk at a party and told me all about the Bain-Harris foundation in Singapore."

"What do you think of it?"

"I think that when that gets out there is going to be one of the most wonderful yakety-yaks this town has heard for years. With everyone looking straight at you, friend."

"I've had that a lot of my life."

"This could turn nasty."

"It's nasty being called a dirty gunrunner."

Archie laughed. "I believe I've put that label on you myself."

"Sure."

"When in fact you were just an idealist taking your thirty-five percent cut?"

"That's right," I said.

"Where have all those South Asia revolutions you sponsored got you?"

"Nowhere."

"Except onto the police records in a few countries."

"It's a compliment to be on the police records. Shows you have initiative and drive."

"It would still sound very bad in court."

"Archie, dear, are you suggesting that I'm going to be tried for killing Ella?"

He didn't answer that one; he sat looking at the tiling near his feet.

"Mitchell has quite a reputation here," he said after a time.

"All Scots have reputations everywhere. It's the one thing we live for. And he's got nothing against me at all, except that I was living here and benefit, apparently, by Ella's death. The fact remains that she kept open house. Almost any man could get to her."

Archie's head jerked up.

"What do you mean?"

47

I pointed.

"That balcony. All you needed was the right key. Ella could have had them mass produced."

"She wasn't a tart!"

"No. But a free woman. Playing for kicks. You know that as well as I do."

"Ella was very discreet in Hong Kong."

"It's a place where you have to be. She was adaptable. She had that stair built."

"I don't like this much."

"Look, Archie, I'm facing facts. It's the kind of situation where you have to. With me in the middle of it. What I felt about Ella personally doesn't come into this right now. She can't be damaged. I can. I'm not kidding myself. Mitchell is looking straight at me. And a lot of other people are going to be following his lead soon."

"With you doing what?"

"Being my usual gay self," I said. "Mitchell can't keep me here. I'll be moving around in Hong Kong. Have you got a nice party for me to go to?"

He looked at me.

"There's a big thing tomorrow. Americans."

"Wangle me in?"

"I suppose I could. But . . ."

"Louise wouldn't like it?"

"That wasn't what I was thinking. We'll pick you up here. About half past six."

I smiled at him. I saw Lia Fan coming down the steps to the pool. She stood on the bottom one, not seeing Archie.

"A Mr. Wong is on the phone, Mr. Harris. He wishes to send flowers."

Archie didn't turn his head.

"It's too early," I said.

4

Heather woke me. A displaced Siamese can pierce through tougher sleep than mine. She was on the wrong side of my bedroom door. I put out a hand for my bedside lamp, clicked it on, and the room stayed dark. I pushed back the bedclothes and walked over to the door in my bare feet. The switch there didn't produce any light either.

I was just going to open the door when Heather gave a shout farther down the passage, by Ella's sealed room. I had a hand on the knob, but I didn't turn it; I listened. Through the open window came the rumble of the sea, enough noise to cover any sound in the house. It was pitch dark out there; no moon. Heather squawked once again, but distantly, a protest against neglect, dismal, angry. The glowing dial of my watch was almost bright. Nearly four. I took the watch off and laid it carefully on a chest of drawers. Then I opened the door.

Out in the corridor with the bedroom door pulled to again, there was no sound, nothing but a padded dark with no breathing in it. I had a plan of the house in my mind now, at least the main portions of it, though there were areas I'd never penetrated. The building wasn't economical of passages—you don't have to be, in a temperate climate—and Yamabushi had wanted his main rooms, even bedrooms, facing south to the view. This meant ambling corridors with tiled floors. You don't make any sound with bare feet on tile floors.

I felt the unbroken police seals on Ella's door with my fingers, then moved over to the study opposite. I was sure all the doors along here had been shut as I passed them to bed, but this one wasn't now. I had to put my arm right out to touch the panels. It was wide back. I stood to one side of the door, holding my breath.

It was a utility room without trimmings. I remembered the layout, desk almost in the middle with an office chair behind it. In the corner a filing cabinet, then the window looking onto a court, then a bookcase and two chairs pushed back and obviously not often used. You could walk right round that desk, and I did, slowly, stopping by the window, which was so dark the bulk of my body would scarcely show. Then I went past the front of the desk, pushing a foot out toward the chairs.

My breathing was light. I used my foot a few times. Anyone packed back against that wall wouldn't be expecting to be touched first by toes. I was ready to duck and dive. But there was nothing at the wall or behind the door.

Heather's screeching could have flushed an intruder out of here. I was certain there was an intruder in this sprawling house, someone who knew enough about the place to turn off the electricity at the main. A good dodge, that. Fix dark as your ally and bring your own light. I hadn't a torch. I didn't want one.

I would have liked a knife. They're useful on a hunt like this, not for a kill, but for that moment when metal touches skin, and the surge of terror from it. You can use the second of your adversary's paralyzing terror, in the dark.

I was the hunter to my quarry waiting somewhere after flight. I had to move against his listening stillness. I kept to walls, with my hand out, my heart beating fast, but not so loud the listener would hear. The hunter's heart has to deal with excitement, but not the pounding of terror. I wanted that terror somewhere else, wanted to use it, to hear a breathing too fast for control.

I heard nothing.

The big pink room wasn't even a shape, just a cave. Tang had drawn the curtains for my evening here, something that hadn't been done before during my stay, huge areas of curtains pulled together in a bid for some kind of coziness. Or perhaps Tang had felt the need to shut out the night beyond. I wondered if he had often pulled those curtains for Ella, but I couldn't see it; the room featured its glass, and the design was for a night spectacular of moon beyond or, failing that, the glow of colored bulbs concealed about the terrace. Why the curtains pulled for me?

There was plenty of room in this cave for my quarry to maneuver, the vast arc of the carpet for his silence if he knew I had come. I decided to let him know that, for he was here. There was nothing to ear or nose or aching eye to tell me this, but I knew. My hand slid along the smooth top of the radiogramophone to an ash tray, just shifting it, a slight flick of sound, but enough in this packed, thick darkness.

I was taut for that movement under silence that can be nothing more than a stirring of air in a closed place, a pricking on the skin of suddenly changed pressures.

I felt nothing.

He would be on the carpet. Even the softest of soles have their hiss for tiles, and he wasn't leaving sanctuary. I had to go to him.

The carpet felt like moss, with a lingering, slightly treacherous oiliness in the wool of its tufts. I moved round its edge. I put the intruder by the central group of furniture, but I couldn't be sure. He might be standing clear of that, for freedom. He might be standing now with a gun in one hand and a torch ready in the other.

51

But it's not easy to fire accurately at the moment you switch on a light. A knife is a better weapon: it doesn't call for that second's calculation; it is more directly an extension of the user's intent, quietly co-operative. And you aren't subconsciously steeling yourself, either, against the crack of sound from the thing in your hand. I wished I'd had a knife.

I touched something with my right foot. Heather screeched. Light was a glittering rod past my eyes. And then the dark was deeper than it had been.

There was a strong smell of whisky. I can tell some malt whiskies with my eyes closed by their smell, but not the popular proprietory blends, which all shout corn. This whisky shouted corn.

Pain in my head was a slow pounding big drum. It was making a noise at the back of my ears, the hidden pain noise in a silence all around. When I groaned, that was something farther from me than the thing inside my ears.

I put my hands on cold tiling to push up and felt glass. The reek was from a broken bottle. I felt something else, too—shallow steps behind me. I wasn't in the sitting room.

When I sat up those talking drums under my skull accelerated tempo for a panic signal, and I found I didn't want to try to stand at all. I put my arms around my knees to fight dizziness, and then the lights came on.

The lights were in the sitting room, beyond an arch, and it was like a suddenly illumined stage set, Ella's pink room glowing, the mural lit, a carnival of color sprung on me from darkness.

Light didn't help the dizziness at all. For a moment I had to shut my eyes. And then I thought that if it was a bit soon for walking I could crawl, and I began to do that, past the shattered glass. I was moving, wobbly as a sick dog, when the music started, a violent battering of sound. It was Lise Berens shouting at me from the speaker:

Happen that man
Comes my way,
I hold him and I say,
"Don't try to get away!"

I looked round the corner of the arch. The room was empty. Then there was a shuffling of feet, and before I could begin to pull myself up by the arch column Kirsty was standing almost above me, her arms holding a wool dressing gown tight to her body and her hair grimly disciplined into huge iron curlers.

"Whisky was the one thing that put my father on his knees, too," she said. "You missed the way to your bed. It's up here."

You wouldn't think it would cheer a policeman particularly to know definitely that he has to hunt for a murderer, but when Mitchell told me about the pathologist's findings he wasn't apologizing for his profession at all. There wasn't even that dog sadness in his eyes. He sat in the sun, smoking, keeping those hood lids dropped as though he was acutely interested in the ant life on the terrace. He wasn't even watching for my reaction to the news that it was unlikely any coroner's jury could find Ella had met an accidental death. Blood-stained froth had been found in the air passages; there were faint traces of this on the pillow the inspector had taken away, and certain organs showed marked venous congestion. She had also taken, or been given, a sizable dose of a commercial barbiturate which could be bought over the counter in many downtown chemists' without a doctor's prescription. No trace of this preparation had been found in Ella's bathroom.

None of this altered my feelings any. I had stared at kippers on my breakfast tray with horror, and the precise symptoms of a hangover continued: queasy stomach and an allergic reaction to strong light. Three cups of coffee had helped, but not much. I still needed my dark glasses. You should always take them off when interviewing the police, but I hadn't.

"You haven't seen a doctor?" Mitchell suggested gently.

"About what?"

"Your accident last night."

"So you've been talking to Kirsty?"

"It's my business."

"No doubt you had a full account?"

"Kirsty feels very strongly about the evils of alcohol. Apparently she's had to live with them all her days."

It occurred to me that it would probably seem a little curious to Mitchell that I should come up with my story about having been coshed only after we had been sitting together for twenty minutes. On the other hand the inspector had clearly been spending quite some time snooping about the place before announcing his presence to me. In fact, he hadn't announced it at all; I had seen him standing beside the pool looking thoughtfully into the water. He had come to me with his pathologist's report by a very roundabout route indeed.

"I was coshed in the room behind us last night by an expert," I said.

I doubt that Mitchell would have shown much surprise if his wife of thirty years or so had suddenly announced that she couldn't stand it any longer and was going off with a Chinese circus tumbler. He put no questions during my account of what happened, only moving to light himself a fresh cigarette. When I had finished he suppressed a spasm of coughing.

"How did your intruder get in?" he asked finally.

"I don't know. The seals were intact on Ella's door—I felt them in the dark. So he didn't come by the balcony. But I shouldn't think getting into a glass house like this would be difficult. I could do it and not leave a trace."

"Really? How?"

"A thin knife. I didn't bring mine with me."

"May I have a look at the back of your head?"

"Certainly."

He took a moment over his inspection. He had gentle fingers, a real mother's touch.

"Hm. Quite an egg."

"Hardly the sort of thing you'd get from dropping sozzled onto a flight of steps."

"Well . . . they have sharp edges. I looked. Mr. Harris, why should the intruder go to all the trouble to stage a debauch scene around your unconscious body?"

I took off the black specs, even though the light hurt.

"If you don't believe my story, Inspector, and I don't think you do, I'm rather discredited as a reliable witness. It makes me the type who would invent an elaborate cover-up for the fact that I'd drunk myself unconscious the night after Ella was murdered."

"Is it in your mind, Mr. Harris, that last night's intruder was Miss Bain's killer?"

"Very much in my mind."

"With no reason for your feeling?"

"None. It's just a feeling."

Mitchell stood with his back to me looking at glitter that I couldn't take even with glasses on again.

"Accepting your story, Mr. Harris, how do you reconstruct this intruder's actions after he coshed you?"

"He hauled me into the passage, arranged me for the accident and then went back for a whisky bottle. Mind you, I don't know why I keep saying 'he.' It could so easily have been a woman."

"The intruder breaks a bottle of whisky beside you. What then?"

"He turns on the light switches. And the gram. He knows the gram will take a moment or two to warm up after the current reaches it. Kirsty will be wakened by that bellowing when the lights are working again. It all worked out just as he planned, including Kirsty's temperance-league conclusions."

"So you believe the intruder knows this house well?"

"Better than I do."

"Hm," Mitchell said. "I think I'll just have a look around."

There was something vaguely ominous in that. I watched him amble through glass doors and disappear. I opened my case, took out a cheroot I didn't want, and forced myself to light it. It was a beautiful morning, but I didn't want to let out any cries of joy about being alive in the middle of it.

I sat there thinking what a fool I'd been to take the initiative last night in the living room. I should have waited against one wall for the first move from my visitor. Instead, I'd had to go padding out onto the carpet like a tourist safari hunter in a blacked-out lion's den. It was just asking to be eaten.

Heather jumped up onto the balustrade.

"You!" I said, with bitterness.

I left the Siamese alone and followed the inspector into the pink room, but he'd moved on. I went over to the drinks cabinet and opened it. Someone had been having a bash at the Ericht Mist I had brought Ella. When you are using a very good whisky that isn't easy to come by, and you're the only one using it, you have more than a vague idea about levels in the bottle. The intruder last night had taken time for a generous double. Somehow that made me angrier.

The phone rang. I just let it, wondering how long it would be before someone else took the thing off the hook. Lia Fan was in the study at her letters again and the inspector was probably cruising near an extension, but that bell went on ringing. The moment I stopped it, ears would join me, the inspector and Lia Fan, possibly Tang in the kitchens. For all I knew, Kirsty might be a phone snooper, too.

It was my co-executor, Winton Peebles, and very much the busy lawyer this morning. A lot of things had come up, and he was just pinned to his desk. He was busy in the afternoon, too. I got the impression that Mr. Peebles had got over an earlier desire to see me quickly and now really didn't want to see me at all if he could help it. He was, in fact, stalling. Lawyers can usually sniff something in the wind quicker than the ordinary blundering citizen.

"Well, let's have dinner together in town," I said.

I could almost hear his dismay. It did something to his breathing.

"Dinner's out, I'm afraid. I'm so sorry, Mr. Harris."

"So am I."

I had scarcely hung up before I wasn't alone. Inspector Mitchell had a great psychic gift for a policeman. He could be doing something in one place and suddenly decide he wanted to be somewhere else, dispatching ahead of him the ectoplasmic shape of his body which he then joined without the fuss of muscular activity. He was standing right there beside me, and I could have sworn he hadn't walked into the room.

"Mr. Harris, what time did you go to bed last night?"

"A little after eleven."

"And you slept?"

"I did. Until the cat woke me. I told you."

"Yes. Kirsty helped you back to your room after your . . . accident?"

"She came along. She didn't exactly help me. It's against her principles to touch a drunk."

"What happened in your room?"

"I went to the bathroom and was sick. For about ten minutes. When I came out Kirsty had gone. But she'd tidied the bed up. I remember that."

"She says she never touched the bed."

"What?"

"She says the bed was waiting, unslept in."

We just looked at each other.

"Mr. Harris, did you by any chance tidy the bed when you got up because the cat was calling?"

"No. Why should I?"

"That makes Kirsty a liar."

"Or me."

Mitchell coughed.

"Do you normally sleep with your window shut?" he asked, when he could.

"Never."

"Did you open it last night some time after eleven?"

"Yes, I'm sure I did."

"Kirsty found it shut and opened it while you were being sick in the bathroom. She thought you'd need fresh air."

"You've got two stories here, Inspector. But we'd both be in the clear if the intruder did that tidy in my room. He was certainly methodical. After all, it had to look as though I'd never been to bed."

"Mr. Harris, my experience of people who break into houses is that they usually have a simple objective and are in a highly jumpy state."

"Maybe, but our man had only an old woman to worry about. He could take his time. In fact I know he did. Helped himself to some Ericht Mist. Must have just swigged it out of the bottle, too."

Mitchell wasn't going to be led up any sidetracks. He asked me if I ever took sleeping drugs.

"No."

"Not at any time? You don't carry them?"

"I wouldn't know the name of a popular brand."

"So that Somnabin means nothing to you?"

"Nothing. Is that what they found in Ella?"

"Yes."

I looked into those brown eyes.

"And now you're going to tell me, Inspector, that you've just found a phial of Somnabin hidden in the lining of my suitcase?"

He shook his head.

"No. I started to get promotion when I gave up looking for the neat clue."

"What were you trying to do then, work up my appetite for lunch?"

"A routine question, Mr. Harris."

Something in his expression, a gone look, told me that Inspector Mitchell was about to be somewhere else. I nearly shouted at him to go by all means, but to use his own legs, not dematerialize in front of me.

Tang repeated my request, as though memorizing it.

"You want newspapers?"

"Yes. Why didn't I get them at breakfast?"

"I forget," he said, saluting his own bad memory with a very slight bow.

He brought me the big official mouthpiece of Hong Kong administrative policy, the opposition sheets which weren't much of an opposition, and a rag which was an English edition in six pages of a Chinese daily published by Wong's uncle, who was one of the local untitled press lords. The colonial office has created a few Oriental Knights Bachelor over the years, but never a Chinese lord, which is a pity. A few characters like the Earl Kang Si of Blue Island in Pearl Water would considerably brighten the British upper chamber and certainly do more to hold together what we've got left than half a dozen Colombo Conferences.

All of the papers had an item on Ella's death. None of them made any noise about it. I wasn't mentioned in the official mouthpiece, was called a house guest by the opposition, and a well-known Singapore businessman by Wong's uncle. But somehow I felt this wasn't all. I remembered my fellow executor's breathing on the telephone.

Lia Fan was churning out those letters still, but this morning she didn't mind being interrupted. She looked at me with interest, taking off those specs to see me better.

"How are you feeling, Mr. Harris?"

"So you got the story? Was it from Kirsty?"

"Tang from Kirsty."

"Like to hear my version?"

"I've been sitting here pining for it."

She was a good listener. At the end she said, "You weren't coshed by Louise MacAndrew anyway."

"Why?"

"She uses a bottle of Chanel Five a week. You can even smell it in the rose garden."

"What do you use?"

Lia Fan smiled. She had very pretty teeth, so white and even they could almost have been taken for a set of British National Health porcelain No. 3.

"Plain soap," she said. And after a moment added, "Does the inspector believe you?"

"I don't think he's decided to yet."

I had the feeling that Lia Fan was almost on my side this morning. She might be a dubious ally, but I needed any I could get the way things were shaping.

"It's now known that Ella was murdered," she told me.

"The inspector told you that?"

"Oh, no. He hasn't been in to see me this morning. It was *Asia New Light*."

"What's that?"

Lia Fan opened a drawer and pulled out a Chinese sheet printed on the kind of paper that smells.

"This is a Communist publication, Mr. Harris. Whenever we want to know the worst in Hong Kong we get this. I'm a regular subscriber. Shall I translate?"

"Please do."

She began to read the black ideographs up and down and from right to left. Her rendering of the characters was brisk, and from the first three the message started to come through loud and clear. The ideograph, even reduced to basic simplicities for the near illiterate, gives wonderful scope for innuendo. I had been staying with rich capitalist playgirl found dead in fabulous south coast love nest after wild Peak New Year party. The police were investigating the circumstances of her death.

I didn't come over as a very desirable house guest either, a suspected murderer in China and a well-known saboteur reactionary in Indonesia. I was also an exploiter of Malaya's toiling masses. It all promised splendid new installments in the following days and made nice reading for a coroner's jury. To say nothing of a later jury after an arrest.

Lia Fan lifted her head.

"It doesn't say anything about Ella being murdered. Not directly."

"It does in a stop press, Mr. Harris." She turned to the front page. "Playgirl slain," she read. "Pathologist's report."

"How the hell could they get hold of that?"

"They get hold of everything, somehow. So it's true?"

"Yes."

"Well," Lia Fan said.

She looked at me carefully.

"Just how much of all that about your past is libelous?"

"Not a lot."

"You mean you couldn't get them on any of this?"

"Not really."

"Who did you kill in China?"

"No one, but I can't prove it. I expect the charge will still be waiting for me if I ever land in Red China again. But I don't intend to."

"Isn't Hong Kong a little too near?" she asked gently.

"That could apply to a lot of people walking around on this island."

"And a number of them get kidnaped."

I told her that wasn't one of my major worries at the moment. She took one of my cigarettes. She was being very friendly. At most times in my life Scots prudence would have dictated a considerable detour around this girl, but I had waked up with a lonely feeling. It still persisted. I also had a small folio of unanswered questions about her.

"Miss Fan, I've some business in town and I'm lunching

61

there. I've a cocktail party tonight, but I could be back from that by around eight. Have dinner with me?"

She wasn't the kind of girl to be made breathless with excitement at an invitation to dine out.

"We could go somewhere quiet." I said, "for the sake of your reputation."

"So considerate of you, Mr. Harris. Quiet little spots are not too easy to find on this island."

"What about one of those floating restaurants? Or are they only for the tourist season?"

"Oh, no, they're better just now. I mean the food is better. And that's a nice idea. Very near here, too. I could come back and meet you after your party. Here about eight."

"It'll make my evening," I said.

"You're so kind." She was smiling. "Ella used to go there quite a lot. Tang will make the arrangements for us. I'll see him. And I'll be waiting for you here about eight."

"You wouldn't rather I picked you up at your home?"

"Oh, no. It's easy for me to come here again."

At the door I said, "Call me Paul, Lia."

"Yes, Paul."

Possibly Inspector Mitchell wasn't going to much like my social day. But the only thing he could do about it was arrest me, and I didn't think he was nearly ready for that. It mightn't even be in the good man's mind. Right now he could be off somewhere snuffing along a hotter trail, though if he'd come on one I'd missed it.

The living room was empty. Ella had a built-in music unit along one wall, an elaborate affair disguised as a piece of light wood furniture with lids. One opened onto the radio, and the others a gram and a tape playback. The Berens record was still sitting on the turntable and I switched it on, muted, almost able to hear Ella saying: "How did you know I liked that so much?" But I'd had enough of Berens. There was a tape fitted, too, and for a moment this just crackled. Then there was laughter, music, the rumble of voices. One came out as a screech: "Ella, go on! Do your Sophie Tucker. Go on!"

I stood there with my hands on the wood front listening to Ella doing her Sophie Tucker. She wasn't doing it very well. I'd heard better performances when she was a few years younger. I could see her giving them, too, belting out "My Kind of Man." It pushed me back, quite a way. For some reason I saw Miguel at a Singapore party, the host who looked as though he should be carrying the drink trays. I switched off.

What the hell was all this? The answer was in a cupboard right in the fitment, tapes in tins, each with a bit of sticking plaster on it, and Ella's label for a piece of her past. What kind of life were you having when you had to tin bits of it for a playback?

The answer was "lonely." I wondered when this had started.

Lia said behind me, "If you don't mind we'll postpone that dinner."

I swung round.

"What's happened?"

"Nothing yet. But it looks like it's going to. When you try to leave this house. There's a false calm down this end. You don't see what's happening up at the road. But I went to find Tang, and I saw all right."

"What's out there?"

"About nine reporters, all with cars, and two policemen keeping them out of the drive. Wherever you go today the newshounds will be right behind you. And that quiet dinner . . . well . . ."

I wanted that little time with Lia.

"We could go by boat," I suggested. "Sampan. Ella has a jetty down there. It could just come in and pick us up. We slide away into the night, and nobody the wiser."

"It can be awfully cold out on the water at this time of year."

"But lovely if the moon is up. It will be. Wrap up well."

"Okay," she said, and laughed.

"Lia, Ella never went in for tape recordings when I knew her."

"Oh, that was a fad. She brought one back from Japan about a year ago. I think it must have been specially made. It was tiny and ran off batteries. Small enough to go in a good-sized handbag. It's in the study, would you like to see it?"

"No."

"She used the thing on people when they didn't know, sometimes."

"Screaming fun," I said. "Like a drink?"

"I'd love it."

She had a practiced thirst. It needed a double gin and not a lot of tonic.

"Ella was good to you," I said. "But you didn't like her."

"Not really."

"Why?"

"Perhaps because she was rich and useless."

"She wasn't useless! She was a damn good business woman."

"Then why didn't she get on with it? I had a fair idea how much business she did. Little flurries twice a year. That's about all it was." She smiled. "It's so hard for the poor to love the rich. We can never learn to be properly grateful."

She went out of the room.

That ache at the top of my neck from a bump in the night had started up again when I went out to get the car. Yamabushi had slipped up with the garage: there wasn't an electronic eye to open the doors when you stood there breathing heavily. They were nicely balanced doors, but they operated manually and made a certain amount of noise. This resulted in a kind of yipping from up there at the gates, and I saw that the two policemen were having their hands full with the reporters. I had to go in, drive the mini out, and get out of the car to shut the doors again.

There was a shout. One of the reporters had broken through

and was streaming down the steep slope toward me, a small figure in a loud sports jacket, bright shirt, tie flying in the wind, and one hand up to hold his pork pie on his head.

"Mr. Harris! Mr. Harris!"

"Who are you?"

"*Asia New Light.*"

"Get to hell out of here!"

"Mr. Harris, you listen to me! We give truth only. We give truth! You speak to me only truths and they are printing."

"Yeah?"

"Honest, Mr. Harris, I give you good deal."

"Take that hand off the door or I give you a punch in the nose."

"You regret this!"

"I wouldn't regret flattening what nose you have."

"Mr. Harris, you listen to me. We speak to many."

I told him that he and his news editor and his publisher were crap merchants. He hung onto the mini door, so I had to detach him. I wasn't gentle. He almost bounced on asphalt.

"Bloody murdering imperialist!"

I lowered the window from inside.

"Even reporters should watch their language."

There was a rush by the others from the gate. I put my hand on the horn and accelerated. The policeman thought I was making a getaway to a private plane. He waved his arms. One of the reporters jumped in front of the mini and then jumped back again. Two others turned and ran for their cars.

In the mirror I could see Asia New Light panting up behind me toward a Volkswagen which was facing the way I was going. The other cars weren't. It was going to be a trial of strength between the products of the Common Market and British Free Enterprise.

The mini hadn't been souped up, but she was game for an emergency. I had her doing sixty in seconds that would have set a testing track record. Then I had to drop down for one of the few real authentic honest-to-goodness Chinese villages left on the island, which meant dogs and children. That's when the Common Market came roaring up behind, not giving a damn about dogs and children. I put the mini away again, whining. The thing behind us was sounding like the take-off of a probe rocket.

I went up a hill. On a straight the Volks gained, but then the twists began, in and out, sharp ones. I held to sixty-eight, not even skidding round on my pram wheels. I could have beaten a Merc, or a Rolls or a big Jag on that road in my little box with the sharp edges filed off. When I got to the first of the houses on the Peak I turned into a tree-lined drive, switched off, and waited for the Volks to roar past. It did. I'll bet that air-cooled motor was hot.

5

I have an affiliation to a Hong Kong club, one of the older ones, which is now integrated with Chinese who are rich enough but in spite of this retains a wonderful air of dear old Queen Victoria and the lost eras of Colonial Expansion. It has high ceilings, pillars with Ionic tops, palms, portraits, marble, and enormous propeller-bladed fans hanging down on rods where you'd expect chandeliers. It also has heating for the cold weather, but marble fights this, and for three months in the year the place has a kind of august chill it would be a pity to monkey with. You expect to be uncomfortable in an institution of this kind, to eat tepid food, and drink tepid drinks. Thousands have done it before you, and there's a kind of roll of honor about somewhere to those members who hung on a long time in spite of the drafts.

I still find myself, when going into a building of this kind in the Far East, wondering what the Japanese had used it for during their occupation, but I didn't need three guesses here. Those venerable palms had seen a lot. And the grand staircases had certainly echoed to the shrill cry of some Mama-san from Tokyo welcoming a Nippon general on his night out from responsibilities to co-prosperity.

Queen Victoria, too, had never been rehung, which was rather a pity because there was an alcove for her on the main landing. It now contained bright plastic flowers arranged with dreadful ingenuity in the inevitable white urn.

I didn't experiment with the smoking room and a drink, for it was past one. The dining room held about eighty citizens who had made their mark locally in one way or another. I would have said that I'd met, at one time or another, about fifteen of these faces, but I was more of a celebrity than I'd thought. At least half the faces appeared to know me.

This wasn't exactly dramatically apparent—the room didn't encourage drama—but at a good many tables there was a clear suggestion of routine interrupted. Spoons stayed in mid-air. Napkins came up in mustache drill. And there was a sudden creeping silence that half dampened down a rumble of food-taking. Some men with backs to me turned. It was the kind of thing Cary Grant has had to put up with for thirty years, only maybe he gets a smile or two. I didn't. Obviously nearly all the important desks in Hong Kong got mimeographed translations every morning of that Chinese sheet which runs all the news that's not fit to print. There was total enlightenment behind the looks I was getting.

The headwaiter had a nice sense of occasion. I was taken on a long safari between tables to a small one under the vast rounded arch of a window and settled between my audience and the world beyond, in plenty of light. A boy suggested melon, but I took mock turtle soup.

In here the cutlery was of the type that needs strong men to lift it, and the spoons came to a point. I've never been able to understand why the Victorians always pointed their soup spoons unless it was to unmask the cad who hadn't had the proper training from his nanny. There is, after all, a helluva lot to be learned from the way a chap handles his spoon, and the English have always doted on social tests of this kind as a means of character rating. Tickle your tonsils with the point and not only are you out for the diplomatic service, you aren't even fit to pay the milk out of your granny's thin purse.

Over mock turtle I began to have the slightly sour feeling that it would gratify a lot of my audience out there if I were to slip up suddenly on my basic table routine and reveal the bounder behind the façade. It was pretty plain that if I'd ever had any pals in Hong Kong they were now looking the other way, or would if there was any suggestion of my nodding toward them. The man who has the newspapers after him in British society doesn't show up again at the club; he leaves for Madeira with a contract to write his memoirs in one of the Sundays, and his old friends are only expected to recognize him when they're wearing holiday shirts. You have to keep some things sacred, damn it, and if you go slack at the club there'll soon be nothing. I should have eaten Chinese. This appearance was preposterous, against the rules, nearly an outrage.

My prospects for raising money in this city had dimmed. Probably the thing to do would be to fly on to Los Angeles to try and interest a tycoon who was disillusioned with television. That is, if I was allowed to fly on anywhere. I thought about Ella, as I ate Australian frozen mutton, and Lia, over prunes and blancmange.

"May I sit down?"

It was Wong of the hairless knees, wearing a colonial city suiting, which is to say not violently conservative but not flashy either. He looked neat, extremely clean, and as though nothing in life would ever take a bite out of his composure.

"I am as sad as you for Ella," he said.

It was the easy candor of the very rich who don't have to watch out for everything. He put both his elbows on the table, which Victoria wouldn't have liked.

"When is the funeral, Mr. Harris?"

"We won't know until after the inquest."

"I see. I ask myself how it could have happened to her."

I didn't say that it is always risky to have a balcony with steps down from it.

69

"I knew her very well, Mr. Harris. She has been extremely kind to me."

"You saw a good deal of her?"

"Oh, yes. I asked her to become my wife."

His eyes were clipped onto my face for a reaction to that. If I showed incredulous disbelief he would work to break it down.

"Mixed marriages don't often last," I said mildly.

"But they must be made to. It must come."

"Agreed. In theory."

He went on watching me.

"Your position in Hong Kong at the moment is not too happy, Mr. Harris."

All I had to do was beg for help and this kind gentleman would arrange to have me put on a junk for Portuguese Macao, which has never extradited anybody in a hundred years. It was a pretty drastic alternative to my present patterns of life alongside British respectability and not the kind of change in my circumstances I'd make except perhaps to avoid a rope. Did Wong really see that rope in my future? I didn't underestimate his intelligence, only suspected his motives in this friendly approach.

"Your uncle's paper was gentle, Mr. Wong. I appreciated that."

"My uncle's paper has only a small circulation, unfortunately."

"You mean it takes the voice from the gutter to rake them in?"

"True," Wong said seriously. He had the look of someone contemplating policy changes when he took control. "You have seen *Asia New Light?*"

"It was translated to me."

"They do not make serious mistakes," he said, not without a suggestion of grimness.

Then he took a small chit pad out of his inner jacket pocket, wrote on it with a gold pen, and pushed the torn-off sheet over to me.

"This number always gets me. Quickly."

"Thanks." I put the paper away. "What do you know of Inspector Mitchell, Mr. Wong?"

"Very clever. A Scotsman."

"Aren't we all?"

He laughed. "You know, it's true for me. If I have a home anywhere, Mr. Harris, it's Edinburgh. I am happy with Scots people. They have big hearts. I found this in Scotland when I was studying. I fell in love with my landlady's daughter."

"She had red hair?"

Wong's was now a face of happy innocence, from times past.

"Yes! I am a sentimental Chinese. At a Burns Night celebration I can weep."

"You have the advantage of me there," I said.

He got up, nodded, and with the eyes of the room on him, walked out. I watched him go with the feeling that his contempt for this place and its contents was complete. I wondered why he used it.

Hong Kong is getting like Manhattan: it can't push out, so it goes up. Pneumatic drills are continually eating away at the carcasses of yesterday's buildings to make room for something with express elevators. If you happened to own your three-story laundry and back cement drying court you sell and retire into the sweet life, and never a worry about automation. But, of course, little Fu Wat never does own the building, so it's the landlords who get the Cadillacs. Like Manhattan. Or London.

A difference remains in that change is a step over about five decades, what was once a Chinese city becoming a property tycoon's arena almost overnight. You walk past steel and concrete which marches up the hill from the harbor, but behind this, fighting against suffocation, are lanes with balconied, peeling plaster façades, and banners, and clutter, packed with people who haven't yet been displaced up to the eighteenth floor. They haven't long to go, though, and a lot of them walk around with an air of unease, as though they know this. Before it's too late the city fathers ought to make a native reservation on ground somewhere that isn't too expensive, so that Hong Kong will always have a Chinatown.

Peebles and Gillespie had offices in one of the buildings that won't be here next summer—eight stories high, but with a lift made of wrought iron that rattled. I got out of this cage just as Diana Hisling came toward it.

Recognition was immediate from my side, but not from hers. She looked at me, and then as I held open a door that could take off your fingers, looked at me again. I was identified. Having done this she didn't want to turn around inside the cage and face me. I could have been the razor killer who was known to be roaming the downtown business district. Her reaction was as plain as that, terror struggling to pull down a screen of control.

I let the door clip shut, but it was practically a minute before she could push the one necessary button and get taken away. She went, looking up, that face under black hair dead white.

The doors along the passage interested me. There was "A. Chang and Company, Oriental Novelties." Across was Mr. Hing Ya, property factor. There was a wholesale shoe operatives, whatever that might be, but absolutely no sign on a door that seemed likely to have closed behind Mrs. Hisling . . . until I came to the lawyer's.

I didn't open it at once, standing there thinking of some things Russell Menzies had said down in Singapore about his Hong Kong agent. None of them had been complimentary. But then lawyers often tie themselves up like this professionally with characters they don't much like.

The reception office had two doors leading to adjacent

rooms, and was equipped with a little railing to keep clients from a work area and a horsehair sofa for them to wait on. It had, for some reason, pictures of steamships round the walls, old steamships, certainly. There was a Eurasian girl sitting behind a long-carriaged typewriter looking at it as if it had been her enemy for some years. There was a sheet of paper fitted, but she wasn't marking it up any.

I went and stood by the fence. The girl didn't have a plaque giving her name. I always provide my secretaries with a plaque; it places them with the firm, giving them a feeling of belonging, and is almost as vital as a Christmas bonus. This girl didn't look as though she had ever had that bonus, either.

"Yes?" She thought about it and then added, "Sir?"

"I've called to see Mr. Peebles."

"Have you an appointment?"

"No."

"What is the nature of your business?"

"Confidential."

She gave me another look, regretting that "sir." "Mr. Peebles doesn't see anyone without an appointment."

"He'll see me."

"What is your name?"

"Paul Harris."

She could read Chinese all right. Her jaw dropped. For a moment I thought she was going to scream. Then she got up and went to a gate in the fence, keeping her eye on me the whole time. She went through a glazed door and shut it. She would have locked it if there had been a key. In a moment sounds came through a glass panel which suggested the ship was sinking. A man opened the door again.

I once had a dentist who was so beautiful it embarrassed me slightly to go to him for a filling. I had a feeling that the male patients should be reserved for the wizened old partner in the next surgery, Adonis left to the girls for swoon sessions under a diamond drill. Then it turned out that my dentist didn't really care for women at all, and as a result of this he got sent back to Holborn under something of a cloud, which shows that nature can be extremely wasteful.

The man in the doorway wasn't as perfect as the dentist, but he was still quite a hunk. As a bit of male cheesecake and wearing no shirt, he would have sold a lot of calendars to bachelor girls. He had a cleft chin and tug 'em ears and the bluest of blue eyes under a tight cap of black curls. He didn't look like the kind of lawyer I'd have wanted to offer a partnership.

The smile I got was a white flash which would have made a film director order a couple of arc lights switched off.

"Mr. Harris! Do come in."

The office was something done over by a man who liked to live with beauty, or at least liked his decorator. It had wall-to-wall carpeting, hide chairs, a reproduction Braque, a bronze thermos flask and lovely lamps. The firm's money had been saved in the reception area.

The hide chair was comfortable. Mr. Peebles was not. He put his desk between us and the light behind him. Then he leaned forward, folding manicured fingers together on a blotter. It was a bit hard on the poor fellow that I'd caught him when he wasn't in conference with a client, and the general atmosphere of the office didn't suggest terrible work pressures.

My chair seemed a little close to the desk and I pushed it back. This let me see Mr. Peebles's feet, his wastepaper basket, which looked empty, a tennis racket in a case, and a bag that was just about the size to contain white shorts, shirt, and rubber-soled shoes. Almost certainly if I'd been twenty minutes later I'd have found this gentleman gone and untraceable. It was possible that he had been detained by an urgent appointment with Diana Hisling.

My appearance had unnerved him, but he was recovering. All his life Winton Peebles had possessed charm as a major asset, and he had learned how to use it. His voice was a masculine baritone, yet mellifluous, a splendid rumble of sound, its effect rather wasted on me, however.

In my experience the successful lawyer in charge of settling up an estate opens negotiations with an allowance of one to two minutes on the life which has been taken from us, then gets down to business. Somewhat to my impatience Winton Peebles extended these lamentations, never exceeding the bounds of good taste over them, but at great pains to indicate a deep respect for Ella. He dwelt on aspects of Ella's character which had never been strikingly apparent to me, one of them her deep concern for good works. Certainly, as we all do, she wished to leave her money sensibly when she died, but I'd seen nothing to suggest that she was likely to give much of it to the poor while she lived. That wasn't her approach to money at all. And this kind of claptrap from a healthy young man whom Ella had clearly chosen for his looks rather than his brains was a shade irritating. The whole thing wasn't quite unctuous, but came damn near it.

Peebles realized in time that I wasn't in full chase after him on this theme, but the drying up still had to be done gracefully, while I waited.

"I came," I said, "to hear about Angus Bain."

The manicured fingers found a cigarette box. I had the feeling that he rationed his smoking carefully but the moment called for one. I lit a cheroot.

"It was really quite extraordinary, Mr. Harris. I didn't know what to make of things at first."

"At first?"

"Yes. Even up to the time I phoned you. A lawyer comes up against people in odd moods, of course, but I'd never had anything quite like this."

"He was very anti me?"

Winton Peebles smiled.

"Very."

He knew a trick or two and could match brevity with brevity.

"Just what did he say?"

"He accused you of undue influence over his sister. And said this had been going on for a long time. It was something he has always tried to fight, he said."

Ella had certainly made a cute Trilby.

"Presumably I had influenced the making of her will?"

"Very much so, Mr. Harris."

"And what did Angus want to do about this?"

"He asked me if I thought he could contest the will."

"He asked *you* that? As an executor of the estate?"

"I've told you, it was a curious interview. To put it mildly."

"In fact you were consulted by Angus Bain, Mr. Peebles?"

"Well, in a way you could put it like that. The whole thing was most irregular and I told him so. But he was shouting away, and I gave him an opinion of sorts."

"Which was?"

"Merely that it wouldn't be easy to prove undue influence. Very far from easy."

I stared.

"Do you mean, Mr. Peebles, that you suggested it was even thinkable?"

He stirred in his chair.

"It wasn't in any way a normal interview. I was trying to quiet him and get him out of here."

"Mr. Peebles." My voice was loud. "As executor of Miss Bain's estate do you think her will could be contested?"

He was staring at his hands.

"I've said . . . I can't give an opinion on that. In the first place, I'm not in a position to."

"What have you not told me yet?"

He looked up then. He was trying to appear much calmer than he was.

"Miss Bain contemplated another will, Mr. Harris. Indeed, she did more than that. She had me draw it up."

I heard a leather desk clock ticking.

"When?"

"Three weeks ago."

"As executor I'd like to see it. As well as the real will."

The inside of the wall safe wasn't as tidy as the office, but it didn't take Peebles long to find what he wanted. He came back with a bundle tied in red tape and pulled from it two documents, as though he knew where they were.

The first was the will I knew about, dated five years before. It was simple enough and clear, for Russell Menzies had drawn it up. There were half a dozen small legacies and one not so small, to Kirsty, the life interest on fifteen thousand pounds. I was left the quarter of a million sterling outright with no qualifying clauses. The residue of the estate, which would be sizable, was all left to Dundee charities. Attached to this will was a codicil, signed and dated two weeks before, leaving fifty thousand pounds free of duty to Eric Hisling.

So she had got around to that. I was glad. It seems to me that ex-husbands can be a worthy cause.

I opened another sheet of stiff paper. It was, as Peebles had said, dated three weeks ago. The contents were the same as in the previous will with two exceptions: Eric Hisling was not mentioned and in place of my name for the quarter of a million was Angus Bain's.

I looked at Peebles.

"Did you tell Angus about this draft of a new will?"

"No! Certainly not. He already knew."

"How?"

"His sister told him."

That surprised me. It surprised me a lot.

"This is a draft, Mr. Peebles. I take it you took it to Ella as that?"

"Yes."

"And what happened?"

"She tore it up."

"Why?"

"I don't really know. Except that she said you were coming and she wanted to talk over the changes she had in mind with you."

"Ella said that?"

"Yes, Mr. Harris."

I tapped the codicil.

"Whatever Ella planned three weeks ago, this shows that two weeks ago she was sticking by the old will. She had this codicil attached to it."

"I quite agree. There was no talk of a legacy to Mr. Hisling at all when we discussed the new will. She came into my office one day and arranged about the codicil here."

"The fact that Ella tore up this new will would seem to indicate clearly, too, that she was sticking by the old one."

"Meantime, yes," Peebles said quietly.

"Just what do you mean by that?"

"I meant that she was doing nothing until she had seen you, Mr. Harris."

"Why did you keep this copy?"

"Just for reference. In case she wanted to return to it. I thought it might save me another draft."

It also represented a nice little piece of evidence of the deceased's uncertainty of mind if Peebles, as an executor, could be persuaded to use it that way. Had Angus come here to try to persuade him to do that? It was an interesting thought. There was nothing, either, to have stopped Winton Peebles typing out the alleged new will form this morning and inserting it among Ella's documents. That, too, was an interesting thought.

"Mr. Peebles, you phoned me yesterday from your partner's

office . . . when Angus was with you. Does your partner know anything about Ella's affairs?"

"No, he doesn't, as a matter of fact. He's away in England on sick leave."

"So you're running the firm at the moment?"

He didn't like that. He sat up straight.

"I am, yes."

"Has Inspector Mitchell been to see you?"

Again Peebles stirred in his chair.

"Yes, this morning. He came to my house while I was still at breakfast."

"You had a long talk?"

"Quite some time."

"Wills came into it, I expect? You told him about Ella's plans to make a new one?"

"I . . . I felt I was obliged to."

Which meant one of two things: either Mitchell had sucked this information out of the pretty boy or Peebles had deliberately put him in the picture. I wasn't in sympathy with my co-executor right then. And I could see how much the inspector must have enjoyed coming to me with the pathologist's report carrying this other bit of news tucked away at the back of his mind.

"Mr. Peebles, when he was here yesterday did Angus Bain say that he was certain I had flown up from Singapore to stop Ella making a new will?"

"That was one of the things he said."

"And you told the inspector?"

"I . . . ah . . . believe I did."

Mitchell was very likely to be out right now looking for Angus Bain. If I was lucky I might get there first, but somehow luck wasn't doing any overtime on my behalf.

I told Peebles that we would start functioning as executors when the inquest was over. I thought there was a slight lift of his eyebrows at this, but he was back inside his charm quickly and came with me into the outer office. I didn't want him to enjoy his tennis that afternoon. I opened the hall door.

"Yesterday was your first meeting with Angus Bain, was it, Mr. Peebles?"

"Ah . . . yes."

A small panic came into his eyes, the look of a man who has told a lie without taking time to think about it.

A telephone call to the central office of the Refugee Relief Agency got an address for Angus Bain over on the mainland beyond Kowloon. I sat out in the open on the ferry, looking at the craft in one of the world's most crowded harbors.

There were plenty of big ships about, but it is the junks you notice, clusters of them along the shore, and hundreds in movement, most of them powered these days, and chugging along, perhaps a good few fitted with my Dolphin engine. I'm proud of that engine. We've sold eleven thousand of them now, and they're pushing small craft along at up to seven knots all the way from the rivers of north China to Hong Kong, also in Borneo and right down past Indonesia as far as Timor. Not a lot of sales in Indonesia, perhaps, but some on the black market there. Our agency in Hong Kong was doing all right, too. I ought to look in and see them if I got the time.

I've done a lot of traveling in power junks. Harris and Company have a fleet of about thirty based on Malaya, from which there is a tidy, steady trading profit, because we go where no one else does for the kind of cargoes that aren't worth the coaster's stopping time. It's been worth our time over the years in a quiet, unobtrusive way. My junks have also been used on other missions about which we didn't want any publicity at all though once or twice we got it. At various times I've lost three boats to Indonesia in what could be called a private war, but I got the crews back home all right.

The ferry was coming in to the landing stage on the Kowloon side. I can never think of Hong Kong as really China, for on the island something else has grown up, so many layers of living covering what the place was originally that it is now completely foreign to the mainland. But this isn't so of the New Territories; they still remain a piece of China sawn off on a line from Mao's jurisdiction, a complete anachronism in a time which has got rid of similar anachronisms almost everywhere else. There used to be plenty of these little foreign pimples along the coast of India but the last of them has gone, as well as most of the ones on Africa, too. But the New Territories are still a piece of the Orient run by Europeans.

It's not something you notice in Kowloon, which is modern and shouts our time, but once you get outside the city you're in China again, a little museum pocket of it, where the villages have no communes and the peasants, now lightly digging still unflooded paddy for the first rice crop, live in the old patterns. My car went fast down a better road than Mao would have built for it, but they were spreading night soil on the fields, and it was the authentic pong of China, as well as Japan.

The workers out there wore straw hats and dark blue denims. They seemed unaware of these Tarmac strips, as though the roads were something that moved around their living without really touching it. None of these were refugees; their ancestors had just happened to be living here before the Opium Wars. The fugitives from something different might come down these roads by the lorry load, but you didn't look at them; why should you? Can a man grow rice for more than his own family?

I saw the refugees soon enough. The place I was making for wasn't one of the bigger camps, but there were plenty of people in it. It moved with people who had probably for years followed the dream of an escape from Mao without realizing that on the other side of escape was a blank wall. The camp

81

had wire round it and, though they could see through, it was their blank wall. They weren't kept in by any force, but if they went out there was no food.

It wasn't really a camp any more, either. It had been once, something for the army, a dreary neatness of Nissen and tar-roofed huts, but these buildings with their shaky permanence were encrusted with parasitic growths of straw matting, of tin, rotting timber, and even cardboard. These were homes. Electric light came into the camp on poles, but the wires stopped by one of the huts near the gate.

I went into one of these huts. In front of a partition, from beyond which came a din of people and babies crying, was a little clear area of about eight feet by six. In it was a table and a chair and a bald European working on a ledger. When he stood up I saw that he was wearing a cassock.

"I'm looking for Angus Bain . . . ah . . . Father . . . ?"

"Call me mister if you like. Though we are an order here. Anglican. A little one of our own. The Brothers of St. Francis Xavier. My name's Pelham. Or Father John."

"I think . . . I must have come to the wrong camp."

"For Angus? Oh, no, he works here. Sit down. You don't mind a box, do you? I'd offer you my chair but it has a wonky leg. Rather a trap, really."

He laughed. He had a determined and just faintly unnerving merriness. I thought of the faces outside, one or two of them lifted to look at me but beyond any real curiosity.

"Is Angus Bain here?"

"I'm pretty sure not today. I haven't seen him. He pops about, you know. He's a young man. I expect he has to get away from all this. It's rather wearing. But my goodness, he can work when he's here. Marvelous with the children, mar-velous."

"The children?"

"Oh, yes, his specialty, you might say. We haven't a great many, though. The poor little beggars don't get here. Sometimes their parents have even left them. It's too awful to think of, really. But then so much is. You see, ours aren't the Yellow Ox crowd with friends on this side."

"Yellow Ox?"

"So you don't live in Hong Kong? That's the escape line, you know. The business. Money paid here in dollars gets your relations out of China. All that sort of thing. Highly organized. But our poor wretches have most of them sneaked along the coast in tiny boats. No one to pay for them. Or feed them when they get here. We try to. It's not easy."

"Who supports you?"

He laughed.

"We beg like mad. All over the place. The Lord's mendicants you might call us. No shame. And precious little organization, either. Still, we get by. Though sometimes I think Heaven could do a little better by us. But then there are so many calls, aren't there?"

I wasn't at ease. Father John beamed at me.

"Are you a friend of Angus's? Extraordinary chap, isn't he? You know, I think sometimes that Our Lord was a little hard on the rich young man he told to go and sell all he had. Presumably the poor chap didn't. And you know, with a little coaxing he might have come to it. It's not easy to part with this world's goods when you've been brought up to think that's all there is. And it hasn't been easy for Angus. After all, he could go where he wanted and live as he liked. This was a sort of experiment for him. Or it started that way. He gave his time at first, himself you might say, but kept his money in the bank. It took him a while to learn to give to the poor."

"Angus is giving you his money?"

"Well, if it isn't his own I can't think where he's getting it. What's your name by the way?"

"Harris. Paul Harris."

"You haven't sat down. That box is quite clean. And we haven't got bugs. It's a fight, but we manage to keep clear.

One thing we have is water and we make the poor beggars wash. Do you know, I got a case of soap for nothing last week out of the manager of a supermarket in Kowloon. I told him I'd say a prayer for him, and he looked at me as though I was some kind of witch doctor. But I walked out with the soap."

I sat down on the box.

"Now what can I do for you, Mr. Harris?"

"I'm over on business . . . concerning his sister."

"Oh, yes, of course. It was she who brought him out here, really. We have her to thank for that. I believe she visited us once."

No time for the papers over here.

"How is the girl?" Father John asked.

"She's dead."

He crossed himself.

"Good gracious me. How perfectly dreadful for poor Angus! When did this happen?"

"Night before last. Has Angus been here since then?"

"I don't know. Not really. We do try to have meals together and function as a community, but it's not easy. And I've been kept here rather. A new batch came in yesterday. I could find out for you. Brother Thomas ought to know. He runs our dispensary."

"It's all right, Father."

"It's not all right for Angus. This will be a frightful blow to him. I think his sister was all he had in the world. Oh, poor chap."

"Father, have you any idea where Angus stays when he isn't here?"

"I always assumed with his sister. We've never discussed the matter. I'm afraid none of us have much time for private lives."

"But he was away for considerable periods?"

"Oh, yes. As long as a week sometimes. I'd always hoped he was having a good time. And a rest. Because all this does take it out of him. You can see he's the nervy sort, you know. Can't throw things off easily. And I don't think he's found faith yet."

I looked at the floorboards. They had been scrubbed with that water which they had plenty of. Then I got up.

"It was good of you to come for Angus. And to let us know, too. Would you like to see the camp before you go?"

"I don't think I'd better take the time now. Father, this may sound terrible, impertinent, but has Angus been giving you large sums?"

He looked at me. He wasn't smiling.

"Are you in some way responsible for Angus's affairs?"

"Not exactly. But I am for his sister's."

"Oh, I see. The Bain money, is that it? Very well, I'll tell you. There have been times in the last six months when we would have been forced to give up here if Angus hadn't come to the rescue. With large amounts. Very large indeed."

"Thank you," I said.

He came with me to the gate. He looked at the note I gave him.

"Oh. This is very handsome of you, Mr. Harris. A considerably better haul than the soap. It may interest you that this will feed twenty for a month. I hope you can afford it? What business are you in?"

"I'm a retired gunrunner," I said.

6

Ella had given me the name of her stockbroker in Hong Kong. Mr. Hok Yew, Jr., was a man I would have gone into partnership with any year. He was about five feet seven, broad faced, with two gold teeth when he smiled, which wasn't too often at first. He almost certainly drove a Jaguar, had many children, a docile wife and a slightly less docile girl friend, was a lapsed Confucian who still said his prayers twice a year, had a four handicap at golf and lived seriously only for stocks and shares. He had clearly read his morning papers and connected my name to them, which accounted for the preliminary caution.

This I broke down by the only approach likely to interest Mr. Hok, complete honesty. I didn't pretend to be functioning as one of Ella's executors as yet, stating flatly that I found myself in an uncomfortable situation which I was trying to ease by some private inquiries while I was still a free agent. He warmed to me. In view of my impending official capacity in the settlement of Ella's estate he decided to waive professional secrecy.

Ella had been a valued if slightly conservative customer. She made her money out of biscuits, not the markets, which is certainly a sounder way to do it. Her income exceeded her large expenditure even after taxes and the difference was carefully invested in nonspeculative stocks designed for low income yield and capital appreciation without undue risk. At least that had been her policy for most of her time in Hong Kong. There had been a change apparent in recent months, however, for as far back as six months. She had started to sell.

"In a big way?" I asked gently.

Hok Yew nodded.

"Yes, even for Miss Bain in a big way. Offhand I would say that she had cashed since last summer something in the region of just under three hundred thousand Hong Kong dollars."

"Good Lord!"

"Yes, I was surprised, too, Mr. Harris. If Miss Bain had been a gambler I would have said that she was building up funds for a big sortie. And that would have interested me personally quite a good deal. I might even have followed her lead. I am a great believer in the intuitive instinct of women. Are you?"

"It's never worked to my advantage."

"A pity. Perhaps you are not kind to women?" He was an urbane little man.

"Didn't you get a hint what the cash was for, Mr. Hok?"

"None at all."

"So it just went to the bank? It would be interesting to know if it's still there."

"Very. For me, Mr. Harris, the thought of money sitting in a bank brings pain."

"It would be a great help to me if I could have dates when most of these sales took place."

"Well, the last one, and by far the biggest, is sharply in my mind. Just two months ago. I sold a block of shares which realized somewhere about two hundred and five thousand dollars less my commission and charges."

I looked at him.

"So that money ought to be in her account still?"

"Unless she has bought a yacht, Mr. Harris. I haven't heard of one."

"There's just one other thing. Did Ella ever speak to you about her brother, Angus Bain?"

"She did more than that. She brought him to me as a client."

He had leaned back in his chair and brought the tips of his fingers together.

"Will you say more than that, Mr. Hok?"

"I shouldn't."

There was a moment's silence, which I broke. "I am a man in a very peculiar position."

"I know."

"Any information I can get about Angus Bain may be of great help."

"Possibly."

I stood.

"Thank you for your help," I said.

When I was at the door he called out, "Just a minute."

I didn't sit down again.

"You could get me in a jam, Mr. Harris."

"I'd try not to."

He stared at the desk. "Angus Bain brought his capital out here. I think all of it. He is unlike his sister. He plays the markets."

"Well?"

Hok Yew smiled. "All my clients play the markets well, Mr. Harris. It is only a question of the degree of risk they wish. I do the rest."

"Angus was willing to take risks?"

The broker nodded.

"Yes. It's been an interesting time on the markets recently. A good deal of movement. I had one or two leads for my more adventurous clients. Mr. Bain took advantage of them. He is considerably the richer as a result."

"You don't have to answer this, Mr. Hok, but what did Angus do with his profits?"

"He showed faith in me by reinvesting them at once."

"In further speculative deals?"

"You could say that."

"I take it that he hasn't banked any profits to your knowledge."

"Mr. Harris, not only has he not banked his profits, but most of his income comes to me. He seems to live on practically nothing, and if he goes on the way he is doing he will be quite a rich man one of these days. You could say that he is in a very happy financial position at the moment."

"You've been a great help," I said.

Hok Yew smiled. "I know. It will worry me when I get home tonight. Good luck to you."

"Thanks."

"And when your present situation has . . . changed, you will remember Hok Yew and partners for Hong Kong investment, eh?"

I went down to the lobby in an express lift, thinking of Angus Bain. Within the compass of an hour I'd had the portrait of a probationer saint and an apprentice money tycoon, both of them clear portraits. It didn't make any sense.

I went into a telephone booth and got Ella's bank, the Hong Kong and Ceylon. It was well after closing time, but the wage slaves were still at work. I asked for whoever handled Ella's affairs there and eventually landed with an assistant manager who was very cautious indeed. I told him that I was an executor acting for the deceased and he eventually agreed to let me in by a locked side door.

I didn't use the Hok Yew approach to this character; it wouldn't have worked. W. Thurling Johnson, Esq., was of the type which has been right in there bearing the burden and heat of Empire for three centuries. And even with the whole proposition no longer economic—except for Hong Kong—and something to liquidate as quickly as is decent, he could never have been the man with the hammer at the forced sale at all. His was a grave, continuing responsibility that would either be cut off by a blood clot or taken with him into one of those terrible English retirements in the rain.

I was received in a paneled office, which looked a real dignitary's sanctuary, and he sat way off behind a desk designed to repel overdraft seekers. Respectability is undoubtedly the rock on which a stable society is built, but a man can wear it and still leave a little piece of human weakness sticking out. W. Thurling Johnson did not. He would be a manager somewhere before long if the right people died in time, and this was clearly the thought he took home with him every night and woke up with every morning.

I presented my nonexistent credentials which he couldn't quite challenge even though he knew a good deal about me. I'd told him on the phone that my co-executor could confirm my mission, knowing full well that Peebles almost certainly wasn't in his office. Mr. Johnson thought my interest in Ella's accounts was premature, which it was, and, though he didn't exactly say this, his reluctance to take any action on my request was a kind of aura surrounding him.

Eventually, however, he had things sent for, which he arranged on a vast blotter in front of him: relics of the deceased's financial activities which in certain circumstances can seem almost pathetic, but didn't here. Ella, still on her mortuary slab, was in this office already embalmed into the beauty of a gloriously solvent death.

Mr. Johnson cleared his throat, peered at his documents, and from them said in a voice designed to chill, "Just exactly what would you like to know, Mr. Harris?"

"My information is that Miss Bain deposited considerable sums in her accounts with you from last summer onwards."

He looked at me over the spectacles he had put on.

"Ah," he said.

"Miss Bain wasn't the sort of person who would have thought a large deposit account with you a good investment. So I conclude that this money went into her current account?"

Mr. Johnson made no noise at all. I continued to bash at it.

"I should guess that at one period recently her current account held somewhere in the region of three hundred thousand dollars."

Mr. Johnson's fingers probed the little books.

"What I would like to know is what withdrawals there were, if any."

He thought a long time and said, "There were withdrawals."

"For large amounts?"

And then quite surprisingly he broke down, as though from a kind of outrage.

"On December fourteenth, last, Miss Bain withdrew two hundred thousand dollars. In cash."

"That's a lot to take home," I said.

"Yes. In notes of one-thousand-dollar denomination."

"Is that in your books?"

He shook his head. "No. That is from memory. The teller . . . well, he asked me to come out. Not, as you will understand, that I had any right or any wish to question what a client intended to do with such a large sum. Far from it. There were, however, certain security considerations. I suggested an escort home."

"And got a dusty answer, Mr. Johnson?"

"You could put it like that if you wished," he admitted.

It was undoubtedly to my advantage that the assistant manager had been considerably put out by that interview with Ella. He still resented a brush-off when all he had intended was to be avuncular. Even now he looked back with half an anger. I pushed on.

"Prior to the big withdrawal had there been smaller but still sizable ones in the months before?"

He looked at his documents again. It was all of a minute before he spoke.

"Yes."

"And do the total withdrawals mean that in a period of

some months Miss Bain had come near to emptying her current account with you?"

"I wouldn't use the word emptying, Mr. Harris."

He mightn't use the word, but that was what Ella had done. In a short period she had taken home in cash close to three hundred thousand dollars. It was a lot of money for housekeeping. And anyway, why not use your checkbook?

This was clearly what Mr. Johnson was thinking, too. We parted without warmth but with as near understanding as was likely between us, and I was discreetly let out that side door again. There was money involved in Ella's death, and not only money tucked into the security of a will, either.

I drove back to the south shore thinking steadily about Angus, that philanthropist who shelled out cash to refugees and that hoarder who even turned over most of his income to swell his capital.

There was only one reporter waiting at the gates to the house, and he was in his car smoking, not able to take action quickly enough. The mini turned sharply into the drive. I saluted the policeman.

I couldn't find a latchkey and rang for Tang. He was the composed sort of servant who gets over his employer's murder in a day or two. He had a smile for me.

"Inspector wants to see you, Mr. Harris."

"He's here?"

"Sure. In study."

I didn't knock on that door; why should I? Mitchell was sitting at Ella's desk. Opposite him, on one of the straightbacked chairs pulled out from the wall, was Kirsty.

"I'll be back later," I said.

"No! Miss Wilson's just going."

Kirsty rose. I held open the door for her, but she didn't acknowledge this or look at me. I shut the door with the feeling that Mitchell was holding something tight, and whatever his day's work had been he was pleased with it.

I didn't take the interviewee's chair; I went and stood by the window.

"You wanted me?"

"Yes. I thought you'd want to know that Miss Bain's brother came to see me today. At my office in town."

"Rather avoiding this house, isn't he?"

"I don't think that's been deliberate."

"I do," I said.

Then I did sit down. I sat and looked at Mitchell.

"Angus has been stuffing you up with what he calls my character, hasn't he, Inspector? That was his purpose in calling to see you."

"He certainly doesn't seem to think a lot of you."

"And were you impressed by Angus Bain?"

"Ah . . . yes, in a way."

"Let's hear the worst."

The inspector responded to that invitation. "He told me a good deal that I knew already . . . that is, about you."

"You've been in touch with the Singapore police, Inspector?"

"Oh, yes."

"I've a friend in the force. I hope you got him?"

"I wouldn't know about that. You've quite a career behind you, Mr. Harris."

"Here it comes again," I said.

"No, I'm not digging into the past. It was what the young man had to say about your relation with his sister which I found interesting. In his view you were a baneful influence, to put it mildly. This was something he had tried to fight for a long time, and failed. Apparently his sister was infatuated with you."

"Nonsense!"

"Mr. Harris, do you deny that there was talk of marriage between you?"

"Only with three whiskies behind us."

"What do you mean by that?"

"I mean, as you know perfectly well, that the Scots have a strong sentimental streak in them which comes out with drink taken. And is forgotten next morning."

"Mr. Harris, were you ever Miss Bain's lover?"

"Never. Did Angus say I had been?"

"Yes."

"He's a nasty little liar. And anyway, he wouldn't know."

"He says his sister told him."

I smiled at Mitchell. "Angus has been saying all the things you wanted to hear, hasn't he?"

"I wasn't prompting him."

"Why should you, when your witness is being so bloody obliging?"

Mitchell was suddenly hot, too. It was agreeable to get an emotional reaction out of him.

"Mr. Harris! You'll admit that your story about your relation with Miss Bain is just a little hard to believe. A platonic friendship lasting for years which never deepened into anything else. It's not usual, is it? A perfectly even keel?"

"Who said anything about an even keel? Ella and I fought like hell sometimes. But I didn't go to bed with her. And the reason I didn't was that I didn't want to. And I'm damn certain she didn't want sex with me, either. But I *did* love her. She was dear to me. Isn't that love, too?"

He lit a cigarette. There was the smallest tremor in the fingers that held the match. That pleased me.

"I am only trying to interpret the facts logically and with common sense."

"I've never believed in common sense, Inspector. It makes for a dull life."

I went across the room. His voice stopped me at the door.

"Are you going out this evening?"

"Yes."

"May I ask where, Mr. Harris?"

"No. When you have the right to curtail my movement, use

it. Till then, hands off. Oh . . . there's just one thing. Will you be seeing Angus Bain? I'd like to send a message, that I'm longing to see him. You might suggest he calls here again. But leaves the lights working this time."

Louise was in something of a state before we arrived at the Hodge stately home, the impeccable control of yesterday replaced by signs of panic. The situation in which she now found herself was so far outside any known bounds of the permissible that she had lost the rules for behavior. It was obvious that in common decency I should have developed a splitting headache at the last minute, and she had gone on hoping for this until the moment she saw me come out from Ella's house dressed like the dapper man about town I'm not. I was wearing a carnation, a flower for Ella.

Louise stared. It was the role of sponsor that was so upsetting. I'm sure she could have managed to be gracious to an old friend of her husband's at a cocktail party, even if he was rapidly coming up as a number-one murder suspect, provided this had involved only one sustained effort with a tiny glass of gin for support. But to bring him was something quite different again. She sat in front beside Archie looking like a woman who has put on and taken off her makeup three times, and is furious about what has happened to her hair.

Archie had taken one look at the carnation and given a slight guffaw. Then we moved off with Louise trying not to notice the reporters at the gate, for Asia New Light was back again after getting in his copy, and he stood by the Volks as we passed, grinning like one of Satan's minions. Then he climbed in his car and followed us. So did another two cars, forming a convoy.

"Who are the Hodges?" I asked from the back.

"He represents about twenty-nine American firms all not doing business with China," Archie said.

Louise didn't move head or drawn lips.

"Very important?"

"God, yes. All the Americans in this city are important. They've never really made use of a British colony like this before. And I should think Harry has a direct line to the Pentagon."

Louise emerged briefly from the glacier.

"Don't be silly, Archie."

"Janie's cute," Archie said. "And a British colony is just the right place for her. She was brought up on horseback in Virginia. The loss of our Empire hurts her more than it does us."

On white steps under what used to be called a porte-cochere I noticed that Louise was visibly trembling. I felt almost ashamed. Perhaps a doctor's wife up on the Peak hasn't an automatically secure position, and Louise had been hard at the old British indoor sport of social climbing played to such delicate rules you scarcely notice it is going on. But that doesn't mean it isn't eating up your life, like an addiction to Bingo.

It was a nice house, British Colonial 1895 period, with much 1960's money lavished on it. The outer hall was really a foyer, with windows over Hong Kong along one wall, and from the decor, which was discreet, came a whisper of money that didn't need cigar smoke to confirm it. I think a lot of rich Americans are good at admitting to being well-heeled without shouting about it. It was a pleasant rich house, discreetly padded against any loud noises from the outside world and a helluva long way from that refugee camp over in Kowloon.

If Harry Hodge was an undercover agent he didn't look like it; he looked like a nice rich man with a good digestion. He shook my hand while hearing my name as though he never paid the slightest attention to any tabloid dirt from Red sources.

Janie wasn't tall, but was so slim she looked it. They make a fine job of a beautiful woman in Virginia. For this occasion she was lacquered smooth, but I could still see her out of that chestnut wig, with her own hair blowing in the wind. She smiled.

"We're delighted you could come." Just enough warmth, not too much, and a peck kiss for Louise.

Polished people. I became just slightly conscious of that carnation.

There must have been all of two hundred guests at that party, clearly an annual get-them-all-off-and-forget-about-it. But the usual beast-bellow of voices was here somehow muted, perhaps because there was enough space. Women had room to stand clear of each other and price dresses. There was also a clear track to the door and reception line. I was conscious again of more eyes on me than my appearance usually warrants. A Chinese boy in white gave me a champagne cocktail and I moved off alone, in the way a man can at a party, smoking my own cigarette and looking for beauty.

Most of this was Chinese. There was a woman in her thirties, and quite content to be there, wearing sea green and emeralds, an unusual stone in the Far East, where girls tend to go for diamonds. She had obviously designed her life carefully in stages and met all her targets with ease. She could now afford calm and a slightly roving eye. I watched her getting the low-down on me from a European with whom she had clearly no serious connection. She turned from this gently, without the suggestion of a smile, those dark eyes saying that she hadn't yet met a killer socially. She was ready to have her attention engaged.

The waiter gave us more champagne while we looked at each other. Our talk was impeccably decorous, and in less than five minutes we moved to a clump of Chinese, one of the men this girl's husband, a film maker. His wife was his most expensive production, and he wanted all the copyright. She was willing to let him go on having this provided he continued to appreciate her market value. A successful marriage,

97

I thought. It's always a pleasure to run into them.

The men were watching me, but with the kind of tolerance success tends to breed. You don't get up there by being conventional below the veneer. In every big man's life there are rooms he wouldn't like to usher the police into. Possibly they were remembering that, and being deliberately amiable.

Mature Chinese have a realism which goes back through four thousand years of adult experience, a cool assessment of living that includes large areas of our prehistory. And sometimes even with their businessmen you're made aware of this, that there's a lot more than the profit motive. They are here, they don't expect to be here long, and that's a good excuse for a nine-course dinner with music.

We began to talk about food. Mr. Li, the film producer, said that the best Chinese cuisine is now available only in Macao under the Portuguese. He had an interesting theory that Macao would survive Hong Kong as one of the last hand-holds of a European power in the Far East. Mr. Li was producing a film over there, at half the cost of Hong Kong, and he had hopes, by keeping his theme historical, of Red China as a market. Mrs. Li stirred a little.

"Will you not come to us for dinner one night?" she asked.

Mr. Li was less keen on the idea than his wife, but he didn't say that he was working late for the next three weeks. I asked to be allowed to get in touch in a day or two, when I knew that I was free. There was a moment of still, polite silence, and during it I looked across the room.

Diana Hisling was standing near a door open for ventilation. She was alone, wearing a red dress, holding a glass of champagne and looking at me. A moment later when I moved toward her the invitation had been canceled. She turned to give me her complete profile, which was a good one, and then leaned forward over a table for cigarettes. I went through the door onto a long roofed porch. It was dusk out there, but electric lights were on in stone lanterns down below. A lawn took up expensive space, and the trees beyond it were a thick barrier with only the skyscraper lights of the city showing above them. A P. & O. liner was coming into harbor through the narrows, its upper decks floodlit. You couldn't see the hills of China that troubled Louise so much.

I waited for her step and turned when I heard it. I couldn't see her face at all against the lit room behind.

"I'm sorry about New Year's Eve," she said. She had a good voice, deep, the kind you would notice in a roomful of people and remember afterward.

"I wouldn't have let us in either, Mrs. Hisling. A lot of Ella's bright ideas were like that."

"Yes, weren't they?" she agreed.

She went to the railing and put her hands on it. I stood there beside her.

"You wondered about seeing me today, Mr. Harris?"

"Yes."

"He could be our lawyer."

"But he isn't?"

"No. We don't have one. Not enough business to interest a lawyer."

"You wanted to know how much Ella had left your husband?"

"You're quite a guesser."

"Did you find out?"

"No. That is . . . I found out there was legacy. But I don't know how much."

"It's fifty thousand pounds, Mrs. Hisling. Duty free."

She put up her hands to her face. It was an odd way to take this kind of news.

"So she's bought us," Diana Hisling said.

"I don't think she meant it that way."

"You'd defend her." The deep voice was bitter. "Eric does, too. And how he will now! I never thought I was going to marry a man who would be so God damned loyal to his first wife. Ella was Ella and you all loved her, didn't you? It didn't matter what she could do to people like me. She had a big generous heart."

"Ella meant to be kind!" I said sharply.

"Oh, I know, I know. Kind to Eric. And what a difference it's going to make. The difference between a good life and a pretty dreary one. How ungrateful I sound."

"Yes," I said.

She turned to me then. "I'm not grateful! It probably sounds crazy to you. I've never known any security, and this is it. Handed to us in a lump. Eric, paid handsomely for services rendered."

"She was fond of him, Mrs. Hisling."

"She owned him, you mean. She never let him go."

I didn't say anything to that. There was truth in it, of course. Ella never did let anyone go.

"Eric won't have to worry about redundancy now," Diana Hisling said. "We can have a villa in the sun in the south of France. And live there with the memory of Ella. Like a life subscription to a magazine. It keeps coming every month. Like those dividend checks. Regular reminders of the loved one."

She began to cry. After a moment she said, "I'm sorry. I can't go back in to that bloody party. Can we get out from this porch? I'll wait in the car. It's the sort of thing I'm always doing. Failing Eric in his big moments. We didn't rate this party last year. But he's had promotion, and we made it. A duty to his career to come. In spite of his grief. For his wife."

"Mrs. Hisling . . ."

"I said, for his wife! Let go of my arm!"

It wasn't difficult to find the car; it was distinctive in a big arc of parked chrome glitter, a battered Hillman kept on for another year, washed on Saturdays by Eric himself. They hadn't expected anyone to steal it, and the doors weren't locked. Diana opened one of them and slid into a front seat.

"Thanks," she said, looking up. "I know you think I'm hysterical. Maybe I am. And you were an odd person to choose for my little scene. The last person."

"Why?"

"Because people like you don't know what people like me have to contend with. The success man. And the flop woman. That's all I've been. One almighty flop."

"What about your work in London?"

Her head jerked up.

"Oh, you've heard about me, have you? Did Ella put you in the picture? That night on the way home, perhaps? She could never understand what had made Eric look at me, after her. A nobody. On the editorial boards of a surprising number of small weeklies, most of them long since fallen flat on their faces. It was like calling to like, with Eric and me. For he's a flop, too."

Her voice had thinned, losing the deep notes. I don't like playing amateur psychiatrist, but it was my guess that Diana was an hysteric subject, or near it. There are worse things than being married to a woman who is a quiet, steady boozer.

Really for Eric I said, "I heard about your husband's promotion."

That made her laugh.

"Oh, yes he got it. After a delay that was considerably longer than decent. And just before he gets the boot, together with the Order of the British Empire. I think they ought to drop these imperial awards, don't you? They're only good for a laugh at a cocktail party. Not that you'd dare admit that in this town. This holy relic of the good old days, stuffed with refugees from our half of the twentieth century. God, how I hate the place."

"You can get out now."

"We will, don't worry."

She switched on a dash light and began to fumble in the glove compartment, producing a packet of cigarettes. She flicked at the wheel of an empty lighter.

I struck a match. Still in its glow she looked up at me. There were tears in her eyes.

"I'm not waiting, Mr. Harris. Tell Eric to get a taxi home. And they'll give you a whisky back in there if you ask for it nicely. I'm sure you need one."

Diana's bent smile let you see the woman she might be if she could quiet down, rather tough, but basically amiable. A little success would have done it. It was probably too late now. It wasn't security she needed at all, but something she had made, whole in her hands. A good marriage would have been enough.

The car was hemmed in, but she got it out with skill, controlling impatience. In the last sweep she braked, looking at me again.

"Mr. Harris, if I knew anything about who killed Ella I wouldn't tell the police."

Gravel spurted from under the tires.

Down near the gate, just out of range of the glow from the house, was a little huddle of men who might have been chauffeurs. There was no one but me in the drive to watch the car go, at least no one to be seen. But I waited after the Hillman's rear lights blinked away, and in less than a minute a car came from somewhere beyond the grounds, accelerating fast. It's curious how you can sense a police car, even at night. Maybe it's something in the way they're driven, with gears rammed home. After all, it's the taxpayer who maintains the things.

Diana wasn't going back to her house alone. I had thought it probable she would be followed. And what a lot Mitchell must have heard if he had been standing in shadow under the veranda while we talked, and later if he had been behind some of the shrubbery near me. Enough to open up a bright new field in his investigations. I felt a little sorry for Diana Hisling. But there was my own neck to consider.

7

The veranda was still empty, this not being the sort of party for smooching couples. Each of the long windows gave me a frame of the crowd inside, and I walked along until I found one enclosing Eric Hisling. He was talking to a plump woman dressed to her husband's standing in the world, and, from the quiet little diamonds, her old man clearly had a plinth all to himself. The woman was giving out minimum amiability for a minute and a half before she moved on. It was all there in mime and smile. And a woman doing that to a man whose hair is now thin on top is something that can make your toes curl. Mine did.

Yet Eric didn't seem to be noticing. He was waving an empty glass in a decidedly un-Colonial Service manner, and when a waiter came up to fill the thing there was no suggestion that Eric disciplined himself where bubbly was concerned, this despite the fact that the matron raised jeweled fingers in a defense against intemperance. Eric looked like a man who suddenly doesn't care any more, who doesn't give one great big damn, and it was a surprising way for him to look. While I watched he somehow conveyed to the matron that he didn't think she was important, and she took this news badly, glaring for a moment before swiveling away as he fumbled for a cigarette case to offer her.

103

This left him with his glass in one hand and case in the other. He emptied the glass and put it down, then looked at the case as though it was an object long with him for which he hadn't the slightest sentimental affection. He put one cigarette in his mouth, the remaining two in his pocket, and popped the case in a wastepaper basket. Straightening he looked through glass at me.

For a moment drink held him in his private elation and then, quite slowly, his still lean face went flabby. I thought for a moment he was going to make a lunge into the crowd for cover, but I had underestimated his courage. He stepped over to the windows, turned both handles down, and was with me. He remembered, too, to close the doors behind him.

"What the hell do you think you're doing, Harris?"

"Standing here considering my own interests. We all have to."

"Why were you staring at me?"

"You interest me, Eric. Top of the world, aren't you? Don't think I've seen you quite like this before. Actually, I was a bit surprised to see you at this party."

"What do you mean by that?"

He swayed just a little. His back was to the light and I couldn't see his face now.

"Well . . . bereaved ex-husband. It isn't exactly as if you'd cut all connections with Ella, from what I've heard. Mind you, I'm not being censorious. Emily Post doesn't say anything about how we should observe mourning for a divorced spouse. Somebody ought to rewrite the etiquette books for our time, don't you think?"

"You bloody bastard!"

An earlier slight warmth toward this man had been an abstraction. I wasn't feeling it now.

"Your wife has gone home," I said. "She asked me to tell you."

"You . . . were talking to Diana?"

"She more or less forced it on me. She was looking for information. Which you had withheld. I filled in the gap. The amount. Fifty thousand quid. What you're celebrating."

He wanted badly to hit me then. Drink almost gave him the courage.

"Are you saying I knew?"

"Yes."

"You're a damn liar!"

"Don't shout, Eric. There's a window open down there. How often did you visit Ella at her house?"

"What? Her house? I never went there. I swear I never went near the place."

"Ella made a point of telling me that, too. I didn't believe her. And I don't believe you. No doubt you've got rid of the key?"

"Key? I never . . . I don't know what you're talking about."

"Tell that to the police. They're onto the legacy. In fact, you could say they're onto you. Via your wife at the moment. Which is perhaps why you'd better get home. Pity to leave her to face them alone. She was a bit hysterical. She might say anything. She isn't glad about the money, for some reason. Perhaps she can't move into the gold cigarette case world as easily as you."

"My God! You're working this up! To save your own neck. What have you told the police?"

"Not a damn thing. But I'm fighting out of a corner, Eric. Why should I be gentle to you? Go on, tell me."

He didn't say anything. He was a shape against the windows of a party. I didn't have any sense of threat from Eric, just a totally negative reaction, but his stillness was interesting. The champagne had stopped work in him, quite suddenly.

"When you're phoning for a taxi," I said, "order one for me, too."

He still hadn't moved when I went into the party again.

Archie MacAndrew wasn't exactly the social type, but he could use an occasion like this for his own ends, which were increasing the list of his patients. After all, the poor fellow couldn't advertise, only produce a kind of rock-hard charm which made women in particular quite ready to put their life in his hands, and at his rates. He was also the part owner of a fifty-bed nursing home and keeping the place full at forty quid a week each was quite a problem, involving a good deal of overtime. I didn't cut in until there was a lull in these semi-professional activities; that is, until a pretty, fat woman who looked as though it was only a matter of time until the carvers got to work had been dragged off by a male to whom she was clearly married.

"Hello," I said. "Nice party."

Archie turned.

"Where the hell have you been?"

"Out on the veranda, saving a lot of people embarrassment. And I won't stay long with you. I'm going home now by taxi."

"You're not. You're coming to dinner with us."

"Thanks, but I've got a date."

"Who with?"

"A beautiful and mysterious wench."

"Paul, for God's sake watch out what you're doing. You'll be safer with us."

"Safer, maybe. May I whisper a question?"

He looked suspicious.

"Archie, is Diana Hisling your patient?"

"Yes. Why?"

"I should think she needs sleeping pills most nights. Do you prescribe Somnabin?"

He stared.

"Did you think I'd answer that?"

"No. I just wanted to see the look in your eyes. I'm off."

He caught my arm. "What the hell are you up to?"

"Playing around. Jumping about. And wherever I land there's Mitchell."

"You don't mean he followed you here?"

"I haven't seen him. But there's been the old pricking on my skin. I think a taxi's a good way to get out of here. And I'd like to shake him off for the rest of the evening. I've been working on that. See you at the inquest."

"Oh, doctor!" said one of the women.

I grinned and left. Archie looked furious.

The taxi got me away without any signs of pursuit at all. In the middle of suburbs I stopped it, paid the man double his fare, and told him that if he waited for me he'd get double again. Then I walked down a very quiet street until I saw the car parked on the opposite side of the road from the Hislings' gate. I was certain that Mitchell wasn't in that car, only a driver with no sharp sense of police duty. Still I didn't take any chances and walked past the open gate along a shaded pavement to the next garden. I jumped into it, worked through bushes to the Hisling boundary, and jumped that.

There were plenty of lights on in the house, a whole blaze of them. This made the approach to the garage tricky, an elaborate use of tree-dark patches and then a nipping around past the Hillman which was sitting in the drive. The garage doors were open, and just back from them was the thing I had rather hoped I wouldn't see, a neat little Italian motor scooter. It's a handy way of leaving home at night when you've quite a distance to travel but don't want to let your spouse know you're off. Then I noticed something else. The Vespa had an extra parcel carrier fitted under the handlebars, the sort of thing a woman wants for shopping.

Lia Fan wasn't the kind of girl who could wait in a room with a drinks cabinet without mixing herself something. I saw it wasn't her first, either, from the way she was lying back in a Yamabushi chair.

"Maybe your party was lovely," she said. "But mine's been dull."

"Sorry."

107

"An hour! The sing-song girl gets paid for waiting. I don't."

She got up. I didn't think anyone could get out of those chairs like that, in a single, beautifully balanced movement which said a good deal about well-developed thigh muscles. She stood quite still to let me really appreciate what she had done for our evening.

Lia wasn't wearing a *cheongsam*, though the dress was high necked. It was made of violet silk, and heavy silk at that, with the color tone deepening toward the almost floor-level hem. It would have been a tinted, chaste tube of a dress if it hadn't been for the side slit, borrowed from the Chinese, which went zooming up to well above one knee. Her earrings were amethysts, the real thing, and must have cost all of a paddy coolie's annual income. She certainly looked the secretary with a private income who is only typing because business letters and things like that are such tremendous fun.

"There was only one woman at the party who could come near you," I said.

Lia didn't smile.

"Who?"

"A Madame Li. Something to do with the film business."

"Li Ling, the actress. She could never act. One and a half expressions. And she must be an old hag now."

"She's still holding her own."

"I see," said Lia. Then she smiled. "Of course it's so sensible for an actress to marry a producer. It keeps you in front of the cameras long after the public doesn't want you there. You thought her beautiful?"

"Attractive."

"And that's why you're an hour late?"

"No, I had some business after the party."

"Oh. Well, shall we go? The boatman has been waiting for a long time. I expect he's cold."

"Would you like one for the sampan?"

"No."

I didn't notice the coat until Lia Fan went toward the polar bear window seat. On this was a heap of Russian sables. I'm no expert on furs, but I can usually tell the good ones, even at a distance. This was a good one. Perhaps the fact that it was lying there reminded me of Ella sitting on ocelot, and when Lia put the coat on I knew. It was, like all of Ella's coats, spacious. Lia wrapped it round herself, but there was still lots of fur left.

Maybe I shouldn't have said anything, but damn it all, I was an executor of the estate and sables are a capital asset.

"Nice coat."

Lia looked up at me.

"And a perfect fit. That is, if you like a coat you can move around in inside. I do."

"So did Ella."

"She gave me this."

"Handsome gift."

Lia stroked the fur.

"She had a mink and an ermine and an ocelot. A girl can get bored with sables. And they were three years old."

Lia hadn't been forced to break the bedroom seals to get the coat. Ella had taken me on a tour of the house and opened the door to a vast cupboard, air-conditioned and humidity controlled, for storing furs. It opened off a corridor. It seemed quite likely that the key had been kept in the study. Lia could wear the thing now, but it wasn't going home with her.

Tang escorted us down to the private jetty, shining a big torch though the moon was out and doing a good job. The steps were half cut into rock and about thirty feet below us was the pier. This flanked the promontory, leaving a narrow, deep channel just wide enough to take the day cruiser Ella had, though she told me she didn't take it very often. There was a boat house built against the steps and a marine railway up to it.

The waiting sampan had one man in it, and was powered by

a huge outboard. I was interested in outboards. It was a piece of machinery that my Johore syndicate's factory could produce at a price that would undercut the Americans, if we could buy a license somewhere. The Swedes don't design this type of engine, more's the pity, and it isn't a commercial proposition these days to do a little gentle piracy of someone else's design. Still, I looked hard at that big shining lump on the sampan's stern before I looked at the boatman.

He had pocked cheeks and a big grin. It was an off season for casual hiring, and the man expected a big tip. Maybe he knew that I could leave this point privately only by water, and that grin could have been partly conspiratorial. He was certainly very attentive, treating Lia as something fragile and of value, which isn't the usual line of Chinese males toward their women, even ones in sables.

The boatman had been given careful instructions, too. He didn't start the outboard, but poled us down along past the pier and then shipped the big stern sweep which had been fitted with a side mounting for man power when you didn't want to use the outboard. The only sound was a faint creak as the sweep revolved in its pivot, not nearly loud enough to reach up to the policemen on guard.

Lia and I sat on a rattan-covered seat under a canopy, facing the bow. She was lost in furs.

"Neat getaway," I said.

"Tang is efficient."

"Has Ella had him for long? Or did you find him for her?"

Her head turned. "She lost her houseboy. I found Tang."

"I seem to remember that Ella brought her old boy up from Singapore. Faithful retainer and all that. What happened? Did his grandmother die down there and he had to go back to the funeral?"

"He wanted to go home to his wife," Lia said.

About half a mile away from Ella's point the outboard started up. We could have been a fisherman going home after an evening haul. The outboard made the kind of noise which said it had the power to run a cabin cruiser, but we still didn't seem to be going very fast.

"Do you ever clean your plugs?" I shouted back in my utility Cantonese.

The boatman either didn't get that, or he hadn't heard of plugs. He began to sing against the droning. He was just a water-taxi driver anyway; someone else would do the maintenance.

It took us about forty minutes to get to the floating restaurant. It was one of three still functioning, little islands of light anchored a couple of hundred yards offshore, and very pretty they looked approached from the water, with braziers burning on deck and the shelter canopies beaded with lanterns like jazz-age fringed lampshades. The one we were making for was partly glassed in, which probably meant that you could eat out here even in a gale. Loudspeakers rattled with the kind of music that helps the Chinese digest their food, a sort of torture session for instruments and vocalists.

We were hauled up on deck and almost immediately chose our fish from an attached tank. It gives you rather an odd feeling, if you're a sensitive type, to lean on a rail and end a big fish's span by a pointing finger. I chose a lobster, which is supposed to have a rudimentary nerve system, and then we sat down and drank warm wine. Charcoal from the mainland was red and crackling in an iron network basket at our elbows. Lia slipped out of the sables.

From the next table a mother of six stared at those furs. Her inscrutable Oriental face wore the expression of any woman looking at another who is equipped with the kind of coat that can never be bought out of the housekeeping money. Not that mama was impoverished; you didn't eat out here if you were. She had three diamond rings on one finger and there was probably a Buick waiting for them in the parking lot on shore. Still, children cost a lot, and especially these ones, who kept

111

their bowls almost continually lifted for the shovel into mouth, with occasional spurt forays of chopsticks toward something succulent in the communal platter.

The mysterious Oriental father had slit eyes enlarged by the powerful lenses needed to cope with myopia from overtime. He looked as if he had been gayer once, but had now paid off the mortgage and was just able to meet the annual premiums on a vast, comprehensive, he-thought-of-his-loved-ones life insurance policy. Father ate slowly, chewing with a consideration for his digestive processes that his years demanded. Clearly they all dined out as a family once a week and then went on to the Odeon Picture House afterward.

Lia had been conscious of our neighbors, too. She said, "I don't know what things are coming to when respectable people can't even go to a decent fish restaurant out of season without having to sit next to a foreigner's ornamental piece."

"That's an odd way to rate yourself."

"It's the way she's rating me. Can't you hear her antennae crackling?"

I could, actually.

"Chinese women like that," Lia said, "are a bulwark of democracy in the Far East. They think it means refrigerators, and they want it. It's such a pity for the West that there are only about a couple of million Chinese women like her. And about three hundred million who haven't any hope of a refrigerator. Do you think you can win against three hundred million deprived Chinese women? Or even hold your own?"

"I wouldn't know."

"You're hoping things will last your time?"

"Don't we all?"

"I don't. But then I haven't a refrigerator. And I pinched this coat from Ella's cupboard, as you know well."

"It's a nice dress you're wearing."

"I didn't really come by this dress honestly, either. Mama

112

over there doesn't like the sauce her shrimps are done in. Or maybe it's only me."

I was glad the food arrived then. My lobster was now hot, garnished with garlic and mushrooms in soy and wine. Mama smelt it and worried about whether she had made a mistake with her own entrée. Lia began to eat carp, which I'd always thought purely decorative, but she picked great chunks off bones with chopsticks and showed clear signs of relish.

There is no floor show in a Hong Kong water restaurant, and you don't need one. We were out just beyond one of those floating junk villages that are spattered about the island's coastline. High-pooped junks huddle together for comfort, with outer fragments sometimes detaching themselves to drift away as sails creak up, but leaving always a solid nucleus, teeming with people and children, tacked to the land. Small craft were in orbit about us: water taxis and scavenger sampans, all loitering near those kitchens from which light blazed and succulent smells were aggressive. There weren't any sea birds, I noticed, perhaps because it was night, but more likely because they had learned there were no pickings here. Any cooked fish heads that went over the side were for humans, and three or four operators worked from tiny boats using butterfly nets, catching garbage and hauling it in. One of these was a woman in dark blue trousers and winter jacket, with a face scarred by gouged lines. Sometimes light caught jade ornaments in her ears. There was a baby about two with her, the child cross-legged on floorboards, squalling like a hungry chick in a nest. The woman pulled in her net, dumped the contents out in a heap which she prodded over for a tasty morsel. The baby always got first pick and swallowed without chewing.

"What you want next?" our waiter asked. He had a menu as long as a Chinese epic poem.

"My friend is rather losing his appetite," Lia said in Cantonese. And then she laughed.

It was about half past ten when we left the barge. I got into the sampan first to help Lia down under the canopy. Along the rail late diners watched us. There was a party of Chinese young men about town making a night of it, and one of them called down something which I missed. Lia lifted her head.

"You're the son of an old sow," she said clearly, without shouting it.

"Lia, what the hell?"

"Sit down, Paul. It's all right."

The boatman pushed off.

"What was all that?"

Lia settled herself.

"Oh, he suggested I spend my next free night with him. Want to go back and punch his nose?"

"Yes."

"I like the way you said that. No hesitation. But we'll just go home, thank you. I've had a lot of training in defending my own honor. That is, when I've decided to."

The big outboard was thumping away behind and the lights from the restaurant were fading out. Moon was gone under cloud, and we weren't carrying a light ourselves. I pointed this out.

"What does it matter?" Lia said.

"Look, I've been out more often than I'd like to admit in a boat that ran without lights. But it wasn't taking people home from a restaurant. And I like to go about my lawful pursuits in a conventional way."

"Don't fuss, Paul. I told him not to use a light."

"Well, I'm not having it this way. It only needs one fisherman asleep with lines out on our course to send us all to the bottom. Do you want to swim a mile in pitch dark?"

"I can't swim." She put her hands around inside my jacket. "The boatman can see in the dark. Though I hope not too well."

She laughed. To say I was held is putting it mildly. It was

114

the oldest clinch in the world. We went down into the little well in front of the rattan seat, and for a moment I wondered about the garlic in my supper. Then I wasn't worrying.

It was an odd way to start another kind of fight. I was aware, dimly, of a voice somewhere behind us. Lia tried to hold my head down with fingers dug into my hair. Then someone stepped on my ankle. I kicked with my free foot. There was a grumble of pain before heavy hands came down on my shoulders. I sent an elbow up and back and got another grunt. Lia's voice, very close, shouted in Cantonese.

"Get him off me, you fools! Get him off!"

She didn't sound like anyone's social secretary.

There were three of us in the little well and another up on the rattan seat. I knew because, now on my knees and flailing about, I sideswiped him. We had quite a passenger list for a little boat, with our taximan still back at the outboard which was going all out and shaking us. Not much room to maneuver, either. Lia was using some brightly colored Cantonese that rang out above the bellow of the outboard. She seemed to resent still being involved with me, as though her part ought to be over. Then, realizing that neutrality was useless in a small cockpit, she started pounding at me with closed fists. I took bearings on a guess and smacked her one hard with an open palm, contacting her face all right. But it was the wrong time to enjoy myself. A welt on one ear put me hard against the boat's low coaming, and I needed both hands to keep from going in the water. The thugs went low for my legs, and I kicked out too late. I went up and over and then down. Just before my head went into the sea I saw Lia, in a light from a torch, peering down to supervise this exercise. She wasn't trying to urge moderation.

Holding a man over the bow of a moving boat, with his head just shoved under, is an effective way of washing the fight out of him. The thugs had a leg each and there wasn't a thing I could do to break clear. I couldn't keep my mouth shut, either, and had gone under gasping for air. I saw first a spangle of big, glittering stars, then these began to shrivel and contract. There was a roaring in my ears.

I came round first to the sound of my own heartbeat and then, above that, heard the beat of the big outboard. I was lying along the sampan's bottom, and the gurgling of water was just one plank beyond my ear. Someone struck a match, not to look at me, but for a cigarette. I saw a big naked foot near my face, and then I smelt it, too. There was also some kind of hatch in the floorboards I hadn't noticed before.

My stomach folded over and I lost all of the lobster and a lot of seawater. The naked foot moved just in time. Someone shone a torch on me, but I had my eyes shut and groaned. I felt like that groan, too.

There was Cantonese talk which missed me; I couldn't hear words, though I began to get the impression that my captors were a shade anxious about maybe having overdone the water sedation. The torch kept on me so I groaned again, stiffened my body a little and then, not part of the act, was sick only slightly less effectively than the first time. Fortunately there were cracks in the floorboards.

When the torch went out again I risked lifting my head just a little, looking for Lia Fan. She seemed to be the shape sitting on the rattan seat up in front of me, and was probably enjoying the cruise after a good meal, snugly wrapped in Ella's furs. It was the thought of the girl that started to pump adrenalin into my bloodstream. The glands for this job tend to get a bit sluggish as you grow older, needing a big stimulus. They had it. My only satisfaction in that moment was the thought of the clout I'd given her. It had been a tactical error, but I lay there without anything approaching shame for having hit a woman. Maybe the shame would come later. Right then I'd have liked another chance.

The new sound must have come to me first since, lying there

with an ear to the planking, I was a kind of human sonic device. It began as a dull vibration stronger than the outboard, and in a different tone. It increased, and I recognized the heavy, steady throb of big diesels with plenty of punch now being driven at some speed.

Our crew got the message quite quickly, too. The outboard cut out suddenly, and I was then hemmed in by three bodies, none of them highly washed, pressing themselves down out of sight. All my life I've heard that the Chinese don't like the smell of us, but there have been quite a few occasions on which I could return that dislike, with interest.

Breathing was heavy all around me, and it was the sound of men who aren't happy. They were even beginning to sweat on a chilly night, which was encouraging. I appeared to be forgotten meantime, in a big distraction.

It was soon apparent what it was. The dark night was illumined. And without my having to look up at all, the white glare of that light and the power behind it at once suggested the kind of thing they fit to a police patrol boat. The light was moving, too, looking for something. My thugs had been wise to cut the engine, not only for sound, but because a wake would have been spotted at once. They were gambling that the low shape of a dark boat mightn't show up against the piled-up shoreline.

I could see very well now. And I saw a torch dangling from the hand of a squatting man. It was just within reach if I moved effectively, and he had practically forgotten about that torch, his face up, peering at the movement of a hunting light.

I got the torch. There was just time for a strong white column to go up from our boat before three bodies rolled over onto mine, as though I were the mat in a tumbling act. Being the mat probably saved me. They hit each other more than they hit their victim. From up in her exclusive cockpit Lia screamed orders.

A big naked foot went over my face. The man seemed to be

getting up that way, via a foot on my head. I tried to lift that foot with both my hands and got a kick in the kidneys from someone else.

A moment or two later I was lying on floorboards feeling like someone who has had the small wheel of a steamroller go over him, somehow just contriving to miss the main wheel, and vaguely thankful for this. Maybe I could have moved sooner, but when I did it seemed too soon. I could still feel the imprint of a flat foot on one side of my head, and it wouldn't have surprised me to find my other profile embossed onto floorboards.

There was a great and remarkable stillness in the sampan, but in spite of this it took me quite a little time to realize that I was alone in it. Slowly I pulled myself up and looked over the side, straight into a hot white light which blasted me back again. I lay and listened to the approach-sounds and, once, something from a loudspeaker, but I didn't answer or move. I needed the rest.

Light showed the sampan completely empty. There was this hatch beside me from which the thugs had certainly come, but the lid was on tight and I couldn't somehow see all of them, including Lia, going back down in there to shoot themselves. Which meant they were in the water. Curiosity dragged me over to the side away from the light, and I peered out, not able to see anything at first on a now glittering surface. Then there was something floating, like a patch of dark seaweed.

"Ahoy, there, ahoy!" Not a Scots voice. That was something.

I shut my eyes and kept them that way all through the almost swamping noise of activity around me. None of it was directly my concern anyway, and I was getting my strength back. Quite a lot of me seemed to be in working order. I could hold on with my hands and move my legs.

A voice above me said, "What the devil?"

He was a nice young man with the name of Parr, a lieutenant in the water police and wearing winter uniform. I was rather given the feeling that the good old Navy had turned up again in the nick of time and I called him "Commander," which pleased him.

"Were you in this boat alone . . . ah . . . sir?"

"No, Commander, I had friends. I think they jumped overboard."

"What?"

"I didn't hear splashes. But I wasn't hearing much."

"I say, sir, you look a bit bashed about."

"I am. The natives weren't friendly."

"You mean . . . it happened in this boat? Just now?"

"Oh . . . over quite a stretch of time. But I'll be all right. And meantime, get that light from your ship over the water between us and land. Look for swimming heads. Then I'll draw your attention to something else."

That boy didn't waste time. The light lifted off us and probed toward the shore.

"What were you going to show me, sir?"

"This hatch. The boat has a false bottom. I should have guessed. That outboard couldn't push us above about five knots."

"Good Lord!"

Someone else joined us, Chinese this time. The two of them lifted off the hatch cover and Parr went on his knees, flashing a torch down.

"I say! A Yellow Ox boat. A new dodge, too. Simple little sampan with room enough for eight down below."

I began to pull myself up.

"This is quite a haul for us, sir," Parr said.

"What about the swimmers? Hasn't your light got them? The girl said she couldn't swim."

"Girl?"

"My dinner partner."

"Lord, was this some kind of confidence trick?"

"A little rougher, Commander, but you've got the idea. Will you send your ship in toward shore? That point. I've got a feeling they were making for it."

This boy would get promotion. He sent his ship off and then lowered himself down the hatch. I sat looking toward the shore and thinking of Lia Fan. The girl who couldn't swim was probably now climbing up on rocks. Land was nearer than I had thought, another point, rather like Ella's, sticking out at us, but this one left undisturbed to windblown pines which grew down almost to water level, offering nice dark cover. She would be cold, but not much more, the little bitch. She had her dresses slit up the side not for seduction but for the scissor kick.

A voice sounded out from the patrol's loudspeaker.

"There's something that looks like a mangy bit of fur floating here. Do you want it picked up?"

"Yes!" I shouted for Parr. "That's not a mangy bit of fur. It's Russian sables. And I'm responsible for them. Don't let them get any oil."

8

They did themselves rather well at the water-police base. The room they put me into was clearly the mess, and even with only one light switched on it seemed comfortable. I was given a double whisky and told to wait. I knew what for, but I'd finished the whisky by the time Inspector Mitchell just appeared.

"Well, Mr. Harris."

"Hello. You should have joined us on the ship, Inspector. It was a nice trip. Those things can do thirty knots. As soon as they started to use that radio telephone I was expecting you. Have you caught my dinner partner?"

"No. And the houseboy's gone, too. From Miss Bain's. But we'll round them up."

"Will you? I've a feeling you're up against quite an organization here. In my amateur way I was trying to find out a little about them. You can see how successful I've been."

"Yellow Ox," Mitchell said.

"With a side line in murder and kidnaping probably. Only why involve Ella Bain?"

"I don't quite follow you, Mr. Harris."

"I don't quite follow myself, that's the trouble. But Ella's money is in it somewhere."

"What?"

I'd never seen him startled; at least there was some satisfaction in that. I told him about the money, since he'd find out soon anyway. Surprise made him sit down.

"How much did you say?"

"About three hundred thousand. You can confirm with the bank. Miss Lia Fan is some kind of key. I was trying to turn it by taking her out to dinner. Only it seems she was taking me. Can you get me back to Ella's? I want to go to bed."

"Aye."

We didn't talk in the car; there was a dead silence until we were nearly at the other side of the island.

"Mr. Harris, it might be a good idea if you took things easy in the next few days."

"Are you suggesting house arrest?"

"No, I am not."

"I'm free to travel to the inquest tomorrow on my own?"

"Yes. But I wouldn't play any more games. You were lucky tonight."

"I have been for years. I'm alive."

"I'll be putting an extra two men on guard at the house. They'll be patrolling the grounds."

"I'm not hiring any more sampans, Inspector."

"Nonetheless my men will be patrolling the grounds."

He let me out at the gates, and I walked down the sloping drive alone, thinking about one thing: bed. I had my key, and I used it. I don't know why I didn't switch on the hall light at once; perhaps because I heard something before I was aware of it. At any rate I shut the door quietly and just stood there. Then I began to feel my way forward, a foot out probing for those Yamabushi steps. I was down two lots of these before I saw a glow from the living room, but it wasn't a light switched on.

The room had been given a fireplace to add the interest of rough-hewn stone in a patch to the ceiling, and there was a basket grate neatly filled with logs that would need a blow-torch to light them.

The logs had been removed, but the grate was in use, Kirsty kneeling on the tiles in front of it like an old witch at a secret ritual. She was humped forward over a fire, feeding it with cylinders of tape from Ella's library of yesterday's parties. The tapes burned well, too, with little white explosions to start with, then a smoldering, followed by a lot of black smoke up a virgin chimney.

I switched on the indirect lighting.

"The police checked those, Kirsty. All of them."

She pushed herself up, but a tin slithered out from under one foot and she fell forward before I could reach her, on her face among a lot of empty containers.

I didn't like the way she was breathing at all. The edge of a tin had cut her forehead and blood was coming, but with a frightening slowness, as though there wasn't so much of it in those worn veins. I carried her to the fur sofa and laid her flat on it. Almost at once her eyes opened, and it was Kirsty looking at me without anger or any kind of malevolence, as though she was beyond that in some world of her own, a lost world, a dream except for an old woman who insisted on continuing to live in it. No one else could share that world at all. Ella was the centerpiece, but not an Ella any of her friends would recognize; instead, the child of a fantasy, who might be naughty sometimes but was still little Miss Goodheart who had picked up one or two bad habits like a bottle of whisky a day and male callers late at night. Kirsty's eyes kept on me while she moved down those corridors of forgotten experience, alone with the shadows that can become the only reality when you're very old and have had the last focal point of affection taken from you.

I went over to the drinks cabinet and poured out a decent-sized brandy.

"Medicinal," I said, bringing it back.

"No!"

"Now don't be silly, Kirsty."

"I can . . . take it myself."

"All right."

I knew she didn't want me to touch her, so I didn't, even when she had to claw a hand into the curtain to pull herself up. She drank half the brandy, looking at the floor as she did it, and in a moment or two the waxy pallor left her cheeks. She was getting back into herself again.

Kirsty was tough. She came from a country where if you're once pickled in the winds that howl in from the North Sea you can stand almost anything afterward, go on living past any allotted span. Death is a lot longer in coming up in Angus or Aberdeenshire, for it's a fallacy that palm trees and the sun keep you going; they don't. The brute winds do a better job for longevity.

"Why were you burning those tapes?"

She went on looking at the floor.

"They weren't Miss Ella."

"They were part of her. I knew her, too."

"No! None of you knew her. No!"

"Why do you hate me, Kirsty? Why did you lie to the police about me?"

"I didn't!"

"You're working for Angus, aren't you? Doing what he tells you?"

"No!"

"You never really liked Angus, not in the way you did Ella. But he's the only Bain left to work for. So you're doing what he tells you."

"No!"

"I'll see you to your room now."

"I'll manage myself."

She swung her legs off the sofa, the movement almost spry. She stood without swaying.

"Kirsty, I'd like you to listen to me for a minute. Ella's left you plenty to live on and to buy a house in Scotland. I'm going to make arrangements for you to go back there."

"You'll do nothing for me!"

There was no use arguing. She went slowly across the sitting room, and I let her. I couldn't make use of these moments of her weakness and just watched her go into a dark passage as though in this house she had no need for lights at all. It was a house that was slowly emptying, coming to the end of its use by Ella and those around her. I remembered I hadn't seen the cat for a long time.

My own room looked very neat. It wasn't until I was in the bathroom that I realized how neat. There was nothing of mine on the shelf above the basin, or in the medicine cabinet. The place was ready for the next guest.

So was the bedroom, wardrobe empty, drawers empty, my cases gone, everything gone, not a pin that belonged to me between these walls. I had been neatly swept out and all traces eliminated.

It gives you a bereft feeling suddenly to have no possessions, not even a traveler's possessions. I went out and down corridors to what I thought was Kirsty's room. I still wasn't sure of the door, but I heard weeping.

"Kirsty! What has Tang done with my things?"

When there was no answer I beat on the panels. The weeping went on. Then I heard Heather's voice, a different tone, no despair here, just fury and irritation at being a prisoner. Kirsty had taken Heather and was keeping her. She hadn't much to keep.

I turned away from a locked door.

I went out from a darkened sitting room to a darker terrace

and stood there listening. Mitchell's men were almost certainly patrolling the grounds and as silently as they could. It would have been simple enough to find one of them and ask him to bring up my luggage from the jetty. I was now certain that was where it was, but I wasn't keen on having those packed bags fetched for me and the inspector getting to hear all about it. I'd bring them up myself. Then the kidnap attempt against my person would remain something uncomplicatedly extrovert, just part of Hong Kong's daily violence, and no one could possibly suggest that I had packed up with the intention of leaving the island after a farewell dinner with Lia. That I might be planning on a departure via one of the escape routes hinted at by Wong would be one of the things in Mitchell's many-tracked mind. It was why he had surrounded me by pussyfoot watchers.

Black night was my ally. I don't often forget a path or road I've been over once or twice, for there seems to be a computer corner of my brain constantly making and filing blueprints that are ready for instant recall. A small gift, but a boon in my kind of life, allowing me on occasion to move just that fraction more quietly than the other man, which can mean you don't get a knife in your throat. It meant, in Ella's garden, that I was able to let a policeman walk past so close I could hear his breathing, though he couldn't hear mine. This one was climbing back from what could only have been a patrol down the steps and along the stone jetty.

The boat house was an obvious place to have put my bags. It didn't take me long to get there; the sloshing of water down below was both a guide and a cover for movement. My hands touched the grooved ridges of sliding doors. I felt along for the handles. Under them was a stout mortise lock of the kind that would have stood up to a good deal of vandalism and even held a cracksman for ten minutes. It didn't hold me at all, for the lock was caught back.

A black parlor to walk into, with maybe a spider waiting.

I opened a slice big enough to let me through, the door grumbling only gently on oiled runners. Then I stood inside smelling cigarette smoke.

I wanted light in there. It seemed prudent first to shut the door, and when I had done this, light was provided from a switch by Lia Fan.

She was standing back against a concrete wall, just beyond the looming hull of a stout-looking cabin cruiser. She was wearing men's blue dungarees turned up at the cuffs and a checked flannel shirt much too big for her and unbuttoned for cleavage. She looked tidy, with her hair dry again and combed out. One hand came slowly down from the light switch, but the other kept steadily up in spite of the weight in it. This was a big black Luger fitted with one of those little round box silencers that really do cut down the noise of a bullet sent out.

"For someone who doesn't swim you get where you want to be," I said.

"I'm one of those girls who find it easier to lie. A habit of years. Automatic even when it isn't necessary."

"You'll make some man really happy."

"Probably."

"I could have been a policeman, Lia."

Her hand was still up and still steady.

"I didn't think so. I had a policeman. They always rattle doors. It's part of their training. He found this one locked."

"Then you opened up for me?"

"I thought you'd want your pajamas. And guess where they'd been put. I've been standing at a crack in these doors for a long time now, wondering if you'd gone to bed raw. But don't think I'm tired, Paul. My stamina is remarkable. You often get it in little women."

There was a slight staining of the skin high up on one of Lia's cheekbones. She had just missed developing a black eye from the palm of my hand.

"It's bright in here," I said.

"Don't worry about that. There are no windows. And we aren't staying long."

"You're taking me someplace?"

"That's right, Paul."

"How?"

The gun moved just a little toward the hull of the cruiser, then back to me.

"You mean to launch this? In the dark?"

"It's easy. We do it all the time. Nice little capstan here which shoots the whole boat on its cradle right into deep water. Takes about two minutes before we're under power from the engines."

"So this is another Yellow Ox boat, housed in Ella's garage?"

Lia smiled.

"Would I be right in thinking I'm being taken to Angus Bain?"

"You'd be right," Lia said.

"Why didn't he just call at the house?"

"He wanted you on his ground."

"Where's that?"

"You'll find out, Paul."

"Where are your assistants?"

"I got rid of them. It's just you and me."

"And your arm's getting tired."

"Oh, no. But I can rest it on my hip. I can fire from there, too. It's not easy to do with a Luger but Angus taught me."

"Fancy Angus knowing about guns. When I saw him last he was banning the bomb."

"He's changed, I expect. Angus knows about a lot of things."

"I'm finding that out. When did Ella? Just before she died?"

Lia didn't move. Her face told me nothing at all. It was a flat mask that could have been looking at me from a wall.

"We'll not talk about Ella at the moment," she said. "I want you to move around here a little, toward me. Just a few steps, not too close. Yes, that's right. I'm going up into the cockpit now, but I'll keep you covered all the way. And when I'm up you're going to follow me. Don't make the mistake of thinking I wouldn't use this gun. I've killed a man with it."

"You fancy another notch on the handle?"

"I don't like killing," Lia said.

Then she went up a set of household steps backward, watching me all the time, even as she climbed over into the cockpit. I might have tried diving under the hull, but I think her bullet would have winged me. And I very much wanted to meet Angus Bain, even under escort. I joined Lia in the boat. She had moved back against a canopy upright, in nice Luger range. It wouldn't have been good policy to attempt to get that gun just then.

"You're traveling in the cabin," she said.

"How can you launch this thing without me?"

"The capstan puts her in the water on her cradle. She just floats off it."

"You'll need light to see what you're doing. That'll bring the police."

"They won't get here until we're clear. Go on below, Paul."

"What if I won't?"

"I'll put some lead in your calf as a persuader."

I wasn't prepared right then to gamble that she didn't mean it, especially when the gun lowered. I went toward the open companion hatch, and a quick look at the control panel beside it told me a lot. Underneath us were sealed engines that had cost plenty, operated from a switch like a car's ignition. It might take a moment or two longer than a car to get this boat under way, but it would be a smooth operation. Lia might well have done it on her own before this.

I don't know what made me look through the glass windbreak; there wasn't much to see except the shed roof, the bulk of the cruiser forward, and about four feet of the top of the sliding doors. I stared at them, remembering I'd pulled them shut to a click behind me. They weren't now. There was a one-inch crack.

So I pointed. Before Lia could say anything we both heard the faint grumbling sound as the crack widened to about a foot and a half, just enough to let a man, hidden by the hull, slip into the shed. I heard Lia draw in her breath. She had moved up behind me. I took a long step back, grabbing for her gun arm.

The noise of the Luger was more than a pop, even with its silencer, but a piece of me wasn't torn open. Lia had dropped the gun, but she rallied quickly from shock to put up the performance of a black Mongolian wildcat, even making the snarling noises. It wasn't easy to maneuver her around to the open hatch, and before I got her through it long fingernails had done something unpleasant to one side of my face. Then I got bitten on the wrist. She went below without ceremony and without touching the steps, making quite a noisy landing below in darkness. I shut the hatch and bolted it.

Outside, in the black night, a whistle blew. The policeman had withdrawn to summon reinforcements. I went over the boat's side without bothering about the household steps, landing on concrete with the bent knees of the parachutist who remembers the drill even after being scraped by a tree on the way down. Just behind me, from inside the hull, came a thumping which suggested that Lia hadn't broken any of those frail-looking bones. I didn't get any surge of relief from this.

The whistle out there was being slightly hysterical. Perhaps the sound of the Luger had decided the man to call in his sergeant to direct these operations, and that meant my luck could be in. I pushed one of the sliding doors back, and light flooded down the slipway showing the policeman, still with the whistle in his mouth, caught in a blessed moment of indecision. I got the other door back, running along with it, almost falling over the electric capstan motor. I pulled the handle of this full round, and at once a loud drone filled the shed. Half a minute later the cabin cruiser gave a little jump of surprise and then started off at remarkable speed on its short run down to water. At that moment the policeman decided on a bid for promotion and came for me.

I was just able to keep the trundling boat between us as far as the jetty, where it left me to smack into the water in a cloud of spray followed by a nasty crunching sound as the stern swung around and banged into the jetty. The policeman had worked up a good head of anger and was boiling down on me.

When I'm no longer any use at Malay boxing, I'll retire. It hasn't failed me yet. Part of the act is a bracing of yourself in a bad mime of a character trying to fend off a specialist assault. This is important, for it builds up your opponent's confidence. He then moves in against clearly unskilled resistance and is totally unprepared for a snake foot whipping up for what may be a foul but which works. My man went down flat with his hands thrown out and his head taking stone hard. I turned, ran three yards, and jumped into the cruiser's cockpit.

There was a lot of light from the shed doors and sound from in there, too, an electric motor gone mad and howling. Light came down the steps as well, and was followed by voices. The policeman was pushing himself up onto his knees as I pressed the starter button and lived through that horrid moment of waiting before I could bless sealed Gardiner engines maintained by the makers under guarantee. They rumbled alive.

The cruiser had no line holding her to the land, nothing to cast off, she simply sat waiting up there in the shed for this kind of getaway, balanced on her cradle. I think I established a departure record, easing the boat along parallel to the jetty but leaving as big a gap as I dared with rocks on the other side. Pounding feet pursued, and there were bitter cries of protest.

Armed police could have stopped me, of course, with a couple of well-placed bullets into an exposed cockpit. But this was British China where we govern by the Queensberry rules and a strict system of licensing firearms. It's almost certainly why we still have that toehold on China. Sane people can't understand how we get away with it, believing it must be some kind of subtle come-on when it's just brass neck. The Reds shell Quemoy all the time because Chiang shoots back. He should just sit still and look mysterious. That might even get Khrushchev on his side.

My policeman just had to watch me move past the end of the pier. I thought for a moment he might jump in the water as a keenness gesture, but he decided against this. I switched on the running lights like a respectable citizen, turned west, and gave her the throttle.

The cruiser approved and lifted into speed. I loved that boat at once, just the way she sat on the water, deep enough, not too deep, and the way she rose a little now. The craft shouted good design and marine balance. In this job the money had been put where it mattered, something you don't often get from production-belt models. I once had something like this built in a Fife yard that gets orders from all over the world and deserves them. You can set off from Scotland in forty feet of Fife boat and end up dry in Tahiti. I had a dream of cruising around the thousand Indonesian islands in something I could handle myself, only these days they'd string me up to the nearest palm when I put in for oil and water.

After about a mile due west, just enjoying the boat, I switched off the running lights and turned south. The shed and the jetty had become a glowing blur against darkness, but suddenly, up above, lights began to jump on in Ella's house. That meant telephone calls and police patrols. This time, though, I wasn't in any sampan powered by an outboard. We went up to twenty knots, which is a fair speed on a dark night and a lot more than most cabin cruisers can even think about. I knew now they were twin diesels under my feet, and big ones.

Not a sound came from beyond the hatch doors, which meant that Lia could be quietly busy down there setting up a submachine gun to blast her way out. I decided to give her a little light and pulled down a control panel switch. Then I picked up the Luger. A torch showed me where the bullet had gone, straight into planking, and I hoped without penetration of any tank underneath.

"Lia!"

There was no answer. She might be dying but I didn't think so.

"Lia, what's our course? I need a bearing."

No sound.

"Do you want to deliver me to Angus, or don't you?"

"Go to hell," she said very distinctly.

Her mouth was right up at the crack in the hatch doors.

"All right. I'm due south at the moment. About a mile and a half off Ella's point. On this course we'll be in Borneo in three days."

A good boat cheers me. The wheel had a neat little locking device for the lone sailor out in deep water who wants to go below for a bit of breakfast. I put this on and turned to the hatch, with the Luger ready.

Lia's head was level with my feet; the rest of her stretched down steps into the cabin. She lifted her face and then a hand to push hair out of her eyes. The girl was totally bilingual, but there were moments when English was inadequate for her needs, and this was one of them. She used Cantonese. I let her finish.

"Come on up, like a good girl."

She did, slowly, as though conscious of areas of physical damage.

"Lia, I've taken over this excursion. But I don't know the way to Angus. You steer. It'll give you something to do with your hands. Therapy."

"Bastard," she said.

I threw her cigarettes when I'd lit one for myself, but she ignored them. It was interesting to watch her take over the

133

boat, needing a moment or two to get her own feel for it. Then we began to go faster, which was surprising considering the solid hull.

Lia peered ahead. This gave me her profile in the control panel glow, which was pleasing, the small features of the child she wasn't. The illusion of fragility was there again, and very moving, aesthetically, even when you knew her.

"Where are we going?" I asked.

"Ella's island." She wouldn't look at me.

"Why did Ella want an island?"

"For religious purposes. She met a swami on the plane from Japan. He specialized in giving peace of mind to the rich. You went off some place and stood on your head to let a consciousness of the world ooze out of your ears."

"Ella standing on her head?"

"It makes quite a picture, doesn't it? And it lasted all of three months. During which she built a pavilion on Minshein island. Just a modest little place. All raw wood and discomfort."

"And Angus is out there?"

"That's right."

"Why?"

"He likes it. The fishing's good."

"What happened to the swami?"

"He went on to India to recharge his spiritual batteries. These got run down in the materialist West. For a while Ella and he kept in touch. On an astral level. Then communications got tangled up. It must have been Ella's drinking. You're supposed to eat peanuts and sip water to keep the telepathic lines clear. I think she got tired of the yoga exercises, too."

After a moment Lia added, "The rich have so much time for their souls. The poor just fight the daily battle. Most religions have died of exhaustion in China. Too many empty bellies."

"The new one seems to be catching on."

134

"Mao will have to fill the bellies better than he's doing."

"Are you with Mao?"

That made her turn.

"Me? Why do you think that?"

"Could be you negotiated a good price for handing me over. You and Angus. He seems to be very interested in making money."

Lia was staring ahead again.

"Oh, he is," she agreed. "But we're not selling you to China, if that's any comfort."

"The fact that I'm holding this Luger is more. Look, Lia, I know perfectly well you're mixed up with Yellow Ox, and that's a dirty racket."

"Well, well," she said, turning the boat a little to starboard.

"And you've been using Ella in some way. You and Tang and Angus."

Lia nodded. She was smiling. I could just see the curve of her lips.

"That's right. Using poor Ella. We moved in on her life and made her a puppet who jumped when we jerked the strings. Did she look like that to you?"

Ella hadn't, as a matter of fact. I took another approach.

"Why is Angus on Minshein island tonight?"

"Because he can't get off. We only have this boat and the sampan, and the police have the sampan. I hated taking this boat. We've never wanted the police to notice that it was out in the winter. But they know all about it now."

My head jerked round. There was no mistaking the kind of searchlight mounted on a patrol boat, particularly the kind used to catch illegal immigrants. That light swept low over the water and then lifted to widen its arc. The cockpit about us glowed white.

"They'll have night lenses, too," Lia said. "We are now being chased."

"Quick on the job."

"They prowl all night. You'd think they got a bounty for every poor devil they turn back to China."

"You used that sampan to beat the patrols?"

"Yes."

"What's Angus going to say about losing it?"

"He knows. I called him up on the radiotelephone. We've got one in the cabin. And another on Minshein."

The organization had been quite tidy. Lia could get in touch with her real boss from Ella's house simply by walking down to the boat house. I thought her candor now about this kind of detail was a bit unhealthy, for me.

"They're gaining on us," I told her.

"From the way you say that you'd think the police weren't your friends. Who are your friends, Paul?"

"I count them on four fingers."

"Four? You're lucky."

"Are we going to get away from that patrol?"

"I think so. Haven't you noticed the islands? They're dark, I admit. But we'll be among them in about six minutes. I don't think anyone knows that Ella owned Minshein. It's policy to keep quiet about your yoga hideout. Picnics spoil contemplation."

She lit a cigarette. The spot never left us and the light was whiter. Lia didn't ever look back into it.

"I'm cold, Paul. Make me some coffee."

The cabin wasn't any luxury marine interior; it was very functional, with two bunks, folding table, a two-ring gas plate, a couple of lockers, and a door to the john. In one of the lockers I found my suitcases, so I knew where my pajamas were. There was no hint of armaments beyond the Luger I carried. I had a look at the radiotelephone while the kettle boiled. It wasn't any army surplus and had cost a great deal, with its effective range of about sixty miles. To get that you paid money. It was a piece of equipment I'd always felt I just couldn't afford in my own ships.

The kettle took its time. I hunted round for the builder's plate, which was of good brass and engraved. It said: "Jamieson, boat builders, St. Monance, Fife, Scotland." So my feeling had been right; a Fife boat somehow worked into the Yellow Ox racket, a use that would probably have hurt the feelings of a respectable Scots builder.

"There's a mist down on the islands," Lia called out. "And I'm going to lose the police. They know it, too."

I went up with coffee and a man's sweater from one of the lockers for Lia. I'd left the gun on a bunk below, useless as a symbol of authority. She smiled when she noted this, then wriggled into the sweater. The movement hurt her bottom and she complained of that, in a muffled voice. I asked about her injuries.

"If I'd had a tail it would have been broken off." She looked up at my cheek. "Hm. Nasty! And your wrist?"

"I lost a pint of blood. That's why you've been able to take the initiative again."

Lia reintroduced sex. We were suddenly a man and a girl in a boat, the girl with very long natural eyelashes that could fold down onto a curve of high cheekbone. Hands holding the wheel were tiny, with the nails sheathed. It was all of a minute before I noticed where we were. There was land all around us, great hunks of it, and Lia was pushing that boat up a channel as though it were a train on rails, making for a screen of mist.

Nearly all of China is hungry country, even in the warmer south. The gods mock this with a great deal of totally useless scenic effects. Inland there are areas the size of Texas given over to mountains pinnacled and twisted into near lunatic fancies, a vast acreage of the flamboyantly unusable, where men scratch the ground in shadowed valleys and die. The coastline is decked for thousands of miles with islands that offer nothing for the comfort of man, only tumbled rock and scrub growth, all this the inspiration for the painter on silk. The scroll painters have, through centuries, stubbornly put man against these settings, stylized man who doesn't need to eat, coming down his jadestone path from a red lacquer hermitage half tucked into a cave up behind. The hermit is usually wearing the kind of brilliantly embroidered vestments that would brighten up even a Greek Orthodox ritual; and if he has a vegetable patch somewhere that isn't indicated. Maybe he eats raw puffins. The artists of China until Mao have thumbed their noses at reality, excepting only the poets who have always believed in getting drunk.

We were in one of these pieces of China's scenery. Mist was being slowly whitened by a rising moon, and going into it was like diving into the edge of a huge eiderdown quilt, giving the feeling that softness would at first be resistant, then would split for a suffocating admission. Before mist got us I saw on both sides surrealist landscapes, high dark islands faintly luminous with a significant emptiness.

"For God's sake cut down speed," I shouted.

"I was going to. The mist isn't as thick as it looks. It's all right. And we've lost the patrol. They never come in this channel at all. And certainly won't at night."

"You see a lot of the patrol?"

"They're busy."

"Why don't they land in daytime?"

"Maybe they have. There's only Ella's pavilion. It's sweetly innocent."

"You use this as a refugee staging point?"

"Put your questions to Angus. Any minute now."

It was a good staging point, and the channels between the islands offered all the exits of a well-designed rabbit burrow. A lookout could tell you which way out to use or whether to lie doggo for a few hours more.

Lia spun the wheel and we swung round to port, the boat

138

inching into an anchorage that would have just held a couple of junks, keeping them neatly sheltered by a bulk of land from the prevailing easterly typhoon winds. I could make out a jetty of sorts, gimcrack and picturesque, wobbling down from the island and most of its way pinned to rock. Lia edged toward it, suddenly fussy about a landing, or maybe that the pier wouldn't stand up to much of a bump. I went forward to put over a couple of fenders and then worked my way along the cockpit canopy to have a look at the stern damage. This was mostly to the paint, no planking sprung that I could find. It would take the sea quite a while to break up this boat against rocks.

I got out on the jetty to tie her up, bow and stern, and then noticed that Lia was no longer at the wheel. She was coming up from the cabin with the Luger.

"You forgot this," she said, pointing it at me again.

9

Lia came out from under the cockpit canopy with the gun up.

"I thought we'd stopped playing that game," I said.

"You had. I hadn't."

"Okay, I'm your prisoner again. Great face save. It means a lot to an oriental."

"Shut up, damn you!" The jetty wobbled when she jumped on it.

"Why isn't Angus down to meet us?"

There was just a feeling that this had been troubling Lia, too.

"Walk," she said.

I walked. You had to watch your step. If Ella had built this pier she must have been saving money to spend on her hermitage. It shook, and there were holes in it. The moon behind mist illumination was just about adequate but not more, and I had to keep my head down. In the distance the patrol boat's engines palpitated. Sea birds squawked above us saying they hated visitors late at night. The island felt empty.

A sharp crack of sound first stopped me dead and then put me down on sagging deal planking, flat down, an instinctive reaction from an active life. Someone had a rifle up ahead of us and went on pulling the trigger. The noise smacked down on us, a regular orchestration, the rocks setting up a rowdy sonic amplification, but with no ping of bullets in our area.

When I appreciated this I put up my head and looked back. Like a trained soldier in ambush drill, Lia had gone down on her stomach, but with the gun arm raised and her eyes looking for a target.

"Haven't you got an identification signal?" I asked.

Her answer wasn't at once.

"It's not . . . Angus!"

The rifle began again, and this time we heard it being answered, from what seemed to be a lady's revolver, a little feeble pat of sound against that other purposeful one.

"There's . . . someone else," Lia told me.

"I'd guessed. What do we do? You've got the gun. Would that be Angus with the revolver?"

"I don't know. . . ."

Was Lia frightened? I could scarcely believe it.

"Do you stock rifles on the island?"

"No."

"Then give me the Luger. We'll move."

I got to my knees, testing that, then up. I went back against flanking rock, using it. The mist was tricky, with the slightly unreal effect you often see in the movies but not frequently in fact, drifting along in quite solid patches that might have been propelled by an offstage fan, leaving almost totally clear areas before the next little synthetic cloud. It was a Chinese mist, of the kind a painter would use to make little compartments in his picture. The gaps showed the rocks above us, and I got the rough idea that the island was cleft down the middle by a miniature canyon. The two pieces of high ground couldn't have gone above eight hundred feet, but now they looked like alps on a backdrop, looming and decidedly top-heavy. The fishing might be good out here but nothing would make me use the place for a weekend. And as an island to find your soul in, via yoga, I'd give it a low amenity rating. It was much more likely to lead even a moderately extrovert character straight into the consulting room of one of those top psychiatrists who are always smiling because the resolved life, built up from the subconscious by twenty-five expensive installments, is such a significantly happy thing. In daylight this place might be effective, but I knew that for me it would always keep its feel of nature wanting to stamp on you.

Lia joined me against my slab of stone. She had stopped being aggressive but wasn't using sex. The last echoes of firing had died away. I wondered about the patrol boat hearing the din, but thought it unlikely. It was my guess now that the firing had come from near the canyon, which meant a screen against the sea, and those big diesels set up a lot of noise of their own.

"I suppose you make enemies in the Yellow Ox business?" I said.

"What . . . do you mean?"

"Competitors who think it's easier to shoot you than undercut your price."

From her face, pale in a white mist, that thought went home. Her tongue came out to wet her lips. In between militancy and seduction there was always the child waiting. I took the gun without any resistance. Then we went up the jetty, with the boards making a lot of noise under us, a requiem creaking.

Beyond was a hermit's path beginning with a couple of steps cut into stone and these picturesquely worn down. After that we went up through a particularly horrid stillness with which even the sea birds were now co-operating, watching our feet all the time to keep from kicking stones. I'd put a torch in my pocket, but it wasn't to be risked at the moment. Just behind me Lia was breathing as though she had been exercising. When I stopped, she stopped.

"Can you bring a boat in anywhere besides this anchorage?"

"A small one. There's a beach on the south side. Dangerous with a sea running."

"It's quiet tonight," I said.

We went on. I didn't quite believe in Ella's pavilion when

I saw it. She must have had a phase of looking at Chinese painting. The thing would have made a charming folly in one of those vast English landscaped gardens, with curving tile roof and carved uprights to it, here built to front a cave in the best tradition, an elaborate ornamental façade to Stone Age living. I expected to hear a drip of water and did, from a rivulet in a rock cleft. Ella had come much farther from that Dundee suburb by the silvery Tay than I'd known. As a device to combat alcoholism, her little temple was a shade bizarre.

We went up onto a small porch decorated with freshly painted dragon gingerbread work in wood. There were two round windows with halved round shutters to match, and these were closed. The door was open. In the room I used the torch.

The place had been converted for philistine use. There were sagging wicker chairs and a half-empty tin of baked beans with a spoon sticking out of it sitting on a deal table. Most of the cave had recently been sealed off in hardboard, and against this was an oil stove that could heat you or your tins. I found this still faintly warm to the touch, and on the floor beside it was a pressure lamp with a bent stem and shattered mantle. There was also a small hole in the hardboard, round and quite low.

"Do you remember that?"

Lia shook her head.

"The bullet came through the door. Angus wouldn't try to get out that way. Where's the other exit?"

Lia showed me. The hardboard partition didn't quite make a complete wall; you could get round it at one end and into the cave. This was now a storeroom, with a drum of paraffin and a carton of tinned soup, but nothing really to suggest supplies for refugees and no hint of a radiotelephone.

The cave narrowed, and I began to see the reason for that hardboard windbreak because this wasn't a cave for long; it soon turned into a crevasse down through rock. Above us was sky again, and we walked on bird droppings and some bird bones up a natural ramp which ended in what seemed at first a sheer drop of a hundred feet to the canyon floor below. Then I saw there was a track of sorts down, mostly rudimentary foot- and handholds. Fifteen feet below us, and tucked in behind a boulder that stuck out like a balcony on the cliff face, was a shadowy lump that became human as I stared. It had a face. Before I switched on the torch I knew it was Angus Bain.

His eyes were open, looking straight up. Lia went past me and down. She knew the footholds and almost dropped on the sprawled body.

Then Angus called out, "Lia! For God's sake watch what you're doing. I've broken my leg."

It took us an hour to get Angus down to the cabin cruiser via the cave and the pavilion, most of it with him on my back, and after the first fifteen feet, which were the worst, we got used to the screaming. He wasn't any stoic about pain, which perhaps wasn't surprising since there had been time for shock to wear off and he had a jagged bit of bone sticking out through the flesh of one shin. Lia had the unpleasant job of trying to support the shattered leg in the only position that made him able to endure being moved at all, and once I thought I heard her crying though it seemed a bit out of character. A quick look at the leg in the pavilion decided me that our first aid wouldn't be advisable and the only thing to do was to get him to a doctor as quickly as possible. Angus concurred with this.

"Get me to bloody hell off this damn island."

We got a kind of story out of him, words bubbled through moans of pain. Angus had been sitting by the pressure lamp eating beans when a bullet came through the door. The gunman had made the tactical error of standing too far back, apparently nervous about identification. The muffed shot gave Angus time to sweep the lamp off the table, snatch up a revolver, and run. His idea was to get to the hide for stores and warn Lia on the radiotelephone. But it seemed the gunman

144

knew about the back door and came round through the canyon in time to take another long shot at a man reaching for the first foothold on a cliff face.

The shot was a near miss and not surprisingly Angus lost his hold and fell, landing in the cavity behind the boulder with a leg jerked back up under him. When the pain started he nearly blacked out but was kept conscious by bullets pock-marking the cliff just above. The only real danger to Angus then was a ricochet, and he tried to discourage the killer from coming closer by tugging the revolver from his pocket and pulling the trigger, even though he wasn't aiming at anything. He didn't count his bullets and emptied the chamber. But the killer could have been counting and when there was that long silence which we had shared it suddenly occurred to Angus that the killer could be coming up through the pavilion and the cave for a very simple shot down. It was no wonder I'd seen staring, motionless eyes.

It was while we were still in the pavilion that Lia heard a noise. We went out onto the veranda to listen, leaving Angus on the floor claiming that he was bleeding to death, though the blood wasn't actually bad at all. A boat with a powerful outboard was traveling down the channel beyond the anchorage. These days you can power a speedboat with an outboard, and I was certain I couldn't catch him in the cruiser. So we just listened.

"Lia, when we were getting Angus up to the cave the three of us made a perfect target. He could have picked us off. Did that occur to you at the time?"

"Yes."

"If he's just going away now, he was still around when we did our rescue. Watching us. Why didn't he shoot? A professional killer sent to wipe out opposition would have got his man and anyone else who was around. Why couldn't our gunman play butcher?"

"I don't know." Lia whispered it.

"He might be a friend of yours."

After a moment she said, "I'll go down to the boat for morphine. We keep some in the first-aid box."

Angus was surprisingly stubborn over the morphine, knowing all about dosage. He only allowed Lia to use half an ampoule in the hypodermic; but when we started the portage again, the moaning had diminished, though he was very far from being doped. In the cabin he insisted on having a look at his leg and then was sick on the floor. Lia mopped that up.

I was starting the engines when Angus shouted from below, "Let Lia do it! You can't take this boat out of here. She knows the channels."

Lia came up.

"I think Angus wants to talk to you."

"I'd like to give him the rest of that shot to keep him quiet."

"Please go down."

I took the Luger out of my pocket and laid it above the control panel.

"Let's stop playing who's winning, shall we?"

She nodded.

I had been in fairly close contact with the man down in the cabin for some time without really looking at him, but now I did, sitting on the bunk opposite to do it. I didn't see much change in him. He was still wearing the clothes for the aging beatnik, dirty black pants with one leg cut away above a nasty mess and a black windbreaker over an open-necked shirt which almost certainly served him for pajamas. He had light hair which had never had the courage to go red, and his teeth were a comment on an early neglect of dental drill. Lia couldn't have been weeping. No woman could.

To me Angus had always suggested the small-time actor looking for a really good character part but always kept resting. And the change was here. He had found his part. He mightn't be too good in it, but he had his role now . . . and this was more and more apparent as morphine diminished the pain.

"I could do with a whisky," he said. "The bottle's in that locker."

He held onto a tumbler with both hands, which were small for a man and somehow reminded me of Ella's, well shaped in spite of bitten nails. The boat began to move, and he listened with a certain anxiety, like a trainer pilot who is not very sure of his trainee despite a couple of apparently successful solos. It was a little curious to see Angus worried about something like a boat, but this one was important to him; he'd paid out a good lump of Ella's money for it in cash.

"Lia! That rock to starboard, remember?"

"Yes." She didn't sound too pleased.

"Are you backing out?"

"Yes."

"I thought I'd told you always to turn in here!"

"I'm backing out!"

He finished his whisky.

"How's the pain?" I asked.

"I can stand it now. I guess I made a row. Have you ever broken a leg?"

"Yes."

"Can't it end up with one shorter than the other?"

"Not if you get traction."

"I'm not going into any damn hospital."

"You may have to. And you'd better get some rest now."

"I don't want to rest. I want a refill."

Whisky and morphine didn't sound the sort of combination that would be medically approved, but I let him have it. He looked at me over the glass. I could feel the main channel tugging at us and the engines came out of reverse into half speed ahead. We twisted a little on an ebbing tide that was running fast and then settled. Angus seemed to settle, too. He even smiled.

"How did you like being hijacked?"

"Not much. And it cost you a boat."

"Damn, yes. There hasn't been a boat like that around here

for sixty years. There was once a fleet. Used for knocking off drunken sailors going back to their ships. Sailor hires old woman to take him out. And halfway up come the thugs from the bottom to cosh him, empty his pockets and dump him overboard. It was a regular business, with a lot of drowned sailors as a by-product. The bad old days."

"Who built you that sampan?"

"Oh, just a little boat yard that hasn't lost the old skills. For cash."

Ella's cash.

"Angus, why have you been trying to get me hanged?"

That made him grin.

"Mitchell's got to hang someone. And he won't stumble on the real killer."

"Hadn't it occurred to you that *I* might?"

"It had occurred to me, but you won't. Not without help."

"Do you know who killed your sister?"

"I know who had a very strong motive. And I know where I can lay my hands on a piece of evidence that will turn the heat right off you."

We had propped up his bad leg with pillows, and Angus was staring at a bare knee. Beyond the rumble of the diesels it was very quiet in the cabin. I was conscious of Lia standing up there at the wheel, out of sight, but able to hear us.

"You're not planning to let the police have this evidence?"

"Not at the moment."

He picked up cigarettes from the bunk beside him and lit one. His fingers didn't shake.

"Is there any chance that the killer guesses you have evidence against him?"

"He may."

"You're running quite a risk, aren't you?"

"You've said it."

"What's your game with me, Angus?"

"Simple blackmail."

I had seen this coming but it still winded me. Any discomfort Angus was feeling came from the shattered leg. I had an impression of his total confidence in what he was about.

"I get the evidence for money, is that it?"

"That's it."

"How much?"

"The two hundred and fifty thousand pounds Ella left you. I'd just about persuaded her to put my name for yours."

"My God! You've had plenty from Ella already!"

"Nothing like enough for my needs."

I stared at him.

"Why the hell did you want me on Minshein to put this proposition?"

"My selling price has blurred your perception, Paul. I could have seen you anywhere. But Minshein gave me a chance to put the screws on. I was going to threaten to hold you until after the inquest and then ship you over to Macao. Perhaps now you can see what I was up to?"

I could. Macao is a fugitive's paradise, if he has money. I doubt if it has extradited anyone in the last decade, and it's the place to make for if you're on the run from a Hong Kong embarrassment. To turn up there suddenly would be a kind of brand in itself, no matter how loud a noise you made about your innocence.

Angus was smiling.

"If you'd tried to come back to Hong Kong to defend your honor Mitchell would have stopped playing around and arrested you the moment you landed. And public opinion would have been right behind him. You'd have faced as prejudiced a jury as could be lined up anywhere. I was sure you'd see this clearly, Paul, and pay up. Actually, the kidnaping was an inspiration of the moment. When Lia reported in about a romantic dinner, I was considering various other ways of luring

149

you out here and I think any of them would have worked, because you wanted to see me, didn't you? It's a pity I let Lia lead me into the dramatic. It lost us a good card."

"I'd call it your vital card, Angus."

"Oh, I'll manage without. And you'll pay. Even if I have to wait until Mitchell is really breathing on your neck."

"Mitchell will arrest you for Yellow Ox."

"You think so? Well, a prison hospital would be better than the usual kind. Comfortable and safe. No visiting hours."

Angus had a very good reason for being on Minshein. He had thought it would put him right out of the way of Ella's killer. It must have been a shock to find he hadn't come far enough. It was surprising he wasn't more frightened.

"I could tell Mitchell what you've told me."

"My dear Paul, I'd simply deny it. I've been rather cunning with Mitchell so far."

"You didn't fool him."

"Maybe not. But he'd still use everything that I gave him about you. For one thing, there's a lot to back it up. For another it's his job to put a rope around a neck. The professional policeman doesn't take his doubts home with him. He just likes to have everything neat and tidy."

"That's an old libel."

"It still touches the truth sometimes. And I think it would with the inspector. The man who always gets there. But he won't get Ella's killer without help. It'll be you instead."

After a minute I said, "How did you get your lead to someone else?"

Angus grinned. "Oh, no! I'm not going hand and hand with you up that path. Unless, of course, you want to pay up now? A simple IOU is all I need. I, Paul Harris, promise to pay Angus Bain within three months from this date the sum of two hundred and fifty thousand pounds sterling. I think I'm really being quite reasonable. I'm not asking you for a penny of your own money. Only what you'll get from Ella."

I got up.

"Quite a lot of things have happened to me, Angus, but I've never been blackmailed."

"There's no use telling me I'm an unpleasant character. I've had it all my life, and I'm still not in need of a psychiatrist."

Then he called out to Lia, "What channel are you taking?"

"By Tai Fang island."

"Well, don't! Go out the way you came in. Stick your nose out, switch off the engines, and look and listen. Remember the patrol could be anchored. And shut the hatch so there's no light showing. The ports down here are covered."

Lia shut the hatch.

"That hurt her," Angus said. "Great little eavesdropper. That's one of the things I found useful. Ella didn't tell anyone you were coming. Lia snooped the news."

"Which depressed you?"

"You bet. Just about the last person I wanted to have turn up just then."

Lia opened the hatch a crack. "Where am I supposed to be making for?"

"Ella's point."

"That's going to be nice for me, with the police waiting on the jetty. You want them to take me straight to jail?"

"Everyone's so selfish," Angus said. "Thinking about themselves. Supposing we face up to that problem when we're nearer, eh? Shut that damn hatch!"

"It's one way of getting women to work for you," I said.

"You should try it, Paul."

He was moving into a kind of euphoria from whisky and the drug but still not seeming to lose the sharp edge of consciousness. I'd have to try that combination some time. For my part I was feeling just a little fatigued. I put my feet up.

"That's right, get comfy," Angus said.

He shut his eyes. About ten minutes passed in total silence. I was really tired, with that feeling that if I relaxed into it I'd be sucked into a sodden, almost intoxicated sleep. We heard the engines cut out and the plop of water against the boat's sides. The engines started up again, this time pushed on to almost full speed. Vibration, not usually noticeable, got bad enough to shake me on the bunk.

"I hope she knows what she's doing," Angus said without opening his eyes. "Find out, will you? Put out the cabin light as you go. I like the dark. Oh . . . and leave the hatch open. I'd hate you to try and win her away from me."

Lia had switched off even the control panel light. Cloud had caught the moon and we were being offered a very serviceable darkness, with a faint wind stirring out here clear of the islands. I spotted the patrol boat's light a long way off, half over to Hong Kong, a light following something.

"Were they drawn off after our gunman?"

"Yes." I couldn't see her face. "And they're not going to catch him. Mitchell will be furious about that."

"They'll get his boat. That ought to help."

"I don't think it will. You can hire those speedboats in the harbor. Tourists do it a lot. I'd say he has only to hit land and run for it."

"You've no idea who it was, Lia?"

"Why should I?"

"Yes, why should she?" Angus called up.

In a minute I said, "I've a good idea who the gunman was."

The silence held until Angus laughed. "He's trying to rattle us, Lia."

But I knew she would have liked to see my face then.

I had the wheel as we came in toward Ella's point. It was dark down on the jetty, the boat house lights out, but the house itself looked as though there was a ball on. It was pretty from the sea. Mitchell didn't mind wasting other people's electricity.

Lia came up from the cabin, where I'd heard her whispering with Angus. She stood quite close to me, then reached over to the shelf in front of the windscreen.

"More shooting?" I asked.

Lia just took the gun to the side, and there was enough light to let me see her drop it into the water. I watched her pull the sweater over her head. Sneakers got stuffed in her trouser pockets.

"If you get cramp, don't panic," I said. "Roll over on your back and float."

Lia didn't turn her head. I cut to half speed as she pulled herself up out of the cockpit by the canopy stanchion. The boat wallowed a bit, spoiling a dive which could have been a perfect start to a hundred yards of exhibition crawl. I didn't see her head come up.

"Does that girl always swim out of tight corners?"

Angus had no comment. I gave Lia about five minutes, during which I cut speed; then I switched on the running lights. We came in very respectably and to help us into the channel behind the pier I used the boat's spot, which was a startling blaze of white. There was no reception committee at all. To start things I sounded the klaxon, which made a noise like a 1928 Studebaker two-seater about to pass. With all that rock about, the echoes were very loud indeed.

"What the hell?" Angus shouted.

"You've got to have medical attention right away and I'm not carrying you up those stone stairs."

As I'd expected Mitchell was first onto the jetty, followed with zeal by an assortment of his boys, who had been getting hell from him for some hours. The inspector advanced at the head of his troops. I gave the boat a touch of reverse and then went forward to drop the fenders, after which I picked up the bowline and threw it toward Mitchell. He caught it, after a second's hesitation, and handed it to an assistant. Then he glared.

"I've got Angus Bain down below," I said. "He needs a doctor at once."

Mitchell was maintaining a terrible black Scots silence when

I went back into the cockpit to shut off the engines. We did a feather contact with the pier, which pleased me. The inspector came aboard, but no one else did. I switched on the cabin light for him and after one rather long look at me he went down. Angus let out a terrible moan.

"He's under morphine," I called.

Angus made more noise of a kind which suggested that it would be pretty useless to go through with the formalities of an arrest right then.

"Where's the gurrl?" Mitchell shouted up.

"She didn't come back with us."

"What the hell do you mean? Is she still on the island?"

"I shouldn't think so, now."

"By God, Harris, you'll find it a mistake to play games wi' me."

"If I'd felt you were on my side, Inspector, I wouldn't be trying to."

He came up from the cabin.

"And just what is the meaning of that?"

"I'll be available for questioning when Angus is in the doctor's hands."

"Angus is it now? Suddenly a pal of yours?"

"We're not really close."

"I'm in a position to arrest Angus Bain. Do you have to be told for what?"

"No."

"And yet you've been aiding and abetting him?"

"I've been bringing an injured man back from Minshein island."

"How did you know he was out there?"

"By radiotelephone. It's in the cabin."

"I know it's in the cabin, damn it! I can see. But I left you going to your bed."

"I went for a walk in the garden and saw a light in the boat house."

"You missed my policeman on your walk?"

"Completely."

"But you met up with Miss Fan in the boat house?"

"That's right."

"So you went to Mr. Bain's rescue with the girl you'd got us to look for all over Hong Kong?"

"I didn't really have any choice."

"I see. You mean it was your humanitarian duty to launch this boat and assault a policeman who tried to stop you?"

"I hadn't time to explain the position. Am I under arrest for assault?"

"No, Mr. Harris, not yet. And not for assault."

"I didn't think the force would like the publicity."

Policemen can't use their fists when they want to. Mitchell wanted to. He had to turn away to yap orders up onto the jetty. That sent some of his men scurrying.

"I don't see why we couldn't carry Angus up on the bunk mattress?" I suggested.

Mitchell swiveled to me again.

"This is now a police matter. I'd advise you to do exactly what you're told. And not interfere."

"I think even under the circumstances that Angus Bain has a right to see his own doctor at once."

I really hadn't a leg to stand on here, but I saw Mitchell hesitate. Police regulations haunt them, even when they're senior —that set of rules elaborately designed to protect the public. I pressed things.

"It's possible that he oughtn't to be moved far. He was bleeding badly on the island. It only stopped in the cabin."

The inspector had given up ground and decided to concede it.

"Do you know his doctor?"

"I should think the same as Ella's. MacAndrew. I saw a phone in the boat shed. May I use it?"

"I'll send a man with you."

That might be what I had to expect from now on. I went up the jetty followed by a policeman who turned on the shed lights for me. It was a wall phone and I stood to use it, with the man just behind staring at my back. There was no book, and I didn't remember the surgery number. It took some time to get through via the exchange.

The phone didn't seem to be going to get answered at all; then the burring cut out for Louise's sleepy voice.

"Hello? Hello?"

It was odd that whatever number you rang at a doctor's house gave you Louise.

"This is Paul Harris here. I didn't mean to disturb you. I want Archie."

"He's out. At the nursing home. An emergency. At least I don't think he's in again. He may have forgotten to switch over." The sleepiness went out of her voice. "What's happened?"

"There's been an accident. And I want Archie professionally."

"An accident? At Ella's?"

"No. Not at Ella's. Louise, will you switch over to Archie if he's in?"

"All right. You want him to come to Ella's?"

"Yes. We're here now."

"Who?"

"Will you please get Archie!"

There was a click on the wire, then another sleepy voice, but of a man geared for sudden wakenings to a bell.

"Dr. MacAndrew here."

"Archie, Angus Bain has broken his leg. It's pretty bad. He's here at Ella's now. We need a doctor."

"What? Good Lord, I've only had an hour's sleep. . . ."

"Look, Archie, I just rang your surgery number because we need a doctor. I don't care whether it's you or MacGregor. Tell me his number and I'll ring him."

"No, I'll come."

"You'll find the police buzzing about."

"More than usual?"

"Somewhat," I said.

"Along in twenty minutes."

For some reason I was sweating as I turned from the phone, though it was far from a warm night. The shed lights showed six policemen carrying Angus across the ramp toward the stone steps. They were using the bunk's mattress. To my ears his groans sounded the real thing.

10

Angus was put, with his mattress, on Ella's sitting-room carpet to await the doctor. The journey up had started the bleeding again, and his green look couldn't be acting; the morphine and whisky had worn off. He lay flat on his back with his eyes shut. Mitchell stood over him for a while and then sat down, but still with the air of a policeman ready at any moment to issue the formal warning that goes with an arrest.

Angus opened his eyes and looked at the inspector. "Ah," he said.

"Mr. Bain, are you conscious?"

"Too bloody conscious."

"Then it is my duty to tell you—"

Angus lifted his hand. "Just a minute, Inspector. Spare me the patter."

"I'm obliged to warn you."

"Oh, I know. But you've got me. I can't get away. And I think you ought to hear one or two things. God knows I'm not fit to talk, but you're forcing it on me."

"Talk about what?"

"Just what's going to happen if you arrest me."

"It's my opinion, Mr. Bain, that you will be convicted on

158

the evidence we have. You ran an organization for smuggling illegal immigrants from China into Hong Kong."

"That's perfectly right," Angus agreed, still with his eyes closed.

"You were, in fact, engaged in an activity known locally as Yellow Ox. We have as evidence a boat you used for this purpose, and a search of Minshein island tomorrow will certainly give us more evidence. But more important, we have in custody your man Tang. He has made a full statement."

Angus opened his eyes.

"The clot! How did you get him?"

"He made the mistake of counting on his girl friend to hide him. She decided that this was a poor outlook for her. Sensible girl."

"I'm nicely parceled up. But there's one thing you've missed. Or perhaps Tang never quite understood. He was one of my salaried personnel. And damn well paid, too. The plain fact is, Inspector, that we were not Yellow Ox. That's a dirty, money-making racket. We were a charity."

Mitchell and I both stared.

"A what, Mr. Bain?"

"I think you heard me. A charity. We never made a penny out of running refugees. Much more, we bore all the cost."

"Who is we?"

"My team, Inspector. Why the hell do you think Yellow Ox allowed us to go on operating? That thing is highly organized. The financial backing behind it would probably surprise you."

"It wouldn't," Mitchell said grimly.

"All right, you wouldn't be surprised. But the fact is that if what I was doing had been any threat to Yellow Ox I'd have had my throat cut long ago. They knew what I was up to, and they simply didn't care. Because I didn't touch any of their paying customers. I wasn't undercutting their price; I wasn't taking money at all. Mine were the people who didn't interest them, who hadn't a hope of getting out of China because they hadn't the dollars for the passage. I stuck to the derelicts Yellow Ox wouldn't touch."

Mitchell had a spasm of coughing and through it Angus, whose color hadn't improved, wore an expression of patience.

"Mr. Bain . . . what did you get out of all this?"

"I've told you. Damn all. Now ask me why I did it."

"You've said it was a charity."

"That's what you're arresting, a charity. An organizer of good deeds, for all that they involved law-breaking. But just think of the delicate conscience of Hong Kong about this refugee business, Inspector. The running sore in our buzzing little world. We're in a cleft stick what to do about it, aren't we? And the wretches who get in are not often rounded up and shipped out again. Why? Because of pity. There's still a great deal of pity about. The old-fashioned kind. It's pity that makes men like John Pelham live in a hell hole to fight bugs and hunger. He's an extreme case, maybe. But he's also the conscience of this place. And I was serving that conscience, too, in my own way."

Angus drooped his lids, and they bulged over protruding eyeballs.

"You can arrest me, Inspector. You can bring me to trial. But I think the result would be a howl from the public when all the facts come out. Different if you could show a profit sheet from my activities, but you can't."

After a minute Mitchell said, "You deliberately involved your sister in this business?"

"Yes. I squeezed her for every penny I could get and wanted more. Paul over there will tell you that I didn't use any of my own money. He's been checking up. You'll find I have a sizable capital in Hong Kong I'm trying to increase in every way I can. Ella financed us because I needed my money for the next phase."

The inspector didn't look at me.

"What was the next phase?"

"Getting the sods out of Hong Kong. To stop them rotting here. I need about a million dollars. When I get it the camp in Kowloon won't be a dead end for refugees, just a staging point. They'll move on to some kind of real living."

"Where?" I asked.

Angus's smile was twisted.

"Like to help me, Paul? As yet I don't know. And I've done some looking. But when I have the money I'll find the place. It could be North Borneo. Or an island nobody really wants."

"You mean a major resettlement scheme?"

"I keep telling you! I wasn't major at all; I was minor. Like the old Sunday-school hymn about lighting candles. You in your small corner and me in mine. That kind of stuff. It wasn't much. It was something. I know you're going to find it hard to believe this, Paul. But to me it mattered. God, I'm thirsty. I don't want anything from a bottle. A cup of tea. Where's Kirsty? Why hasn't she shown up? She'd make it."

"Miss Wilson has retired to her room and locked the door," Mitchell said.

"Eh? When did that happen?"

"When we came into the house tonight."

Angus made a sound that was almost a laugh.

"A retirement from the world? Too much happening in it. That's the old for you. First they shut themselves up in a house, then a room, then a bed. Then someone else has to put 'em in a box. But I bet she took food with her. After a certain age all you really care about is your stomach. We all come to it, if we last long enough."

Angus looked first at Mitchell, then at me. He wet his lips.

"Maybe I've been building up too sweet a picture of myself as a humanitarian. I wasn't totally shiny eyed. I didn't bring any of the old people over from Macao. Granny got left on the jetty. You have to make rules, and that was one of mine.

All the people I picked up had to have a working future. When am I going to get that bloody cup of tea?"

"I'll make it," I said, getting up. "You want a policeman to go with me, Inspector?"

Mitchell made no comment. I had never been in the kitchen. It was quite a walk. The house hadn't been built for labor saving at all, and Yamabushi, like most Japanese men, had never spent any time over a hot cook stove. With all that money used up I expected electronic ovens and indirect lighting. What I saw was a square utility room equipped with one of those electric cookers that take their time about doing anything. I sat down on a stool and felt tired. I was still there, the kettle not even murmuring, when the bell rang. They wouldn't hear it in the sitting room, and I took the quick route to the front door.

Archie looked immaculately respectable for the small hours of the morning, dark suit, bag, and all. He seemed surprised to find me playing houseboy. Behind him was the shadow of one of Mitchell's inadequate cops.

"What's all this?" he asked.

"I couldn't begin to tell you—I'd drop off to sleep in the middle. But come in."

I shut the door.

"Angus is in the sitting room lying on a mattress and evading arrest. I think we've all underestimated the boy. He's going to grow up into somebody yet. It's just taken him a long time to get over the natural disadvantages of being rich."

"Where are you going?" Archie asked.

"Back to the kitchen to make tea. Or would you prefer coffee?"

"Tea will do."

He started down the first flight of shallow steps.

"I'm sorry I had to wake Louise," I said.

He half turned.

"You made the startling discovery that I sleep on the ground floor near my surgery? It's been going on for years."

"What's the matter? You snore?"

"Not to my knowledge."

"Well, a ground-floor bedroom with its own exit gives a man a lot of freedom in an old marriage."

"I need it," Archie said and went away from me.

I made tea and gave it the seven minutes to infuse, spending most of that time hunting for biscuits, but Kirsty had got all of them. I did find a chicken in a monster fridge, intact except for the white meat removed from one side. For a while I stared at that chicken wondering if it meant anything to me; then, deciding I wasn't hungry, I just took the tea on a tray set with Yokohama eggshell porcelain.

There was a lot of noise in the sitting room. Angus was telling Archie what he thought about private nursing homes at forty quid a week and that they weren't getting any of his money. Archie was being patient, explaining that a broken leg is scarcely the kind of case for an emergency admission to crowded city hospitals, especially when the patient in question can afford to pay. It wasn't particularly dignified of him, but even the healer has his commercial moments.

"I'll stay here!" Angus shouted. He was assuming now that Mitchell wouldn't resist this suggestion. "You can get me one of your trained nurses."

"Your leg needs to be dealt with in an operating theater."

"That's a lot of crap," Angus yelled. "Any good doctor ought to be able to fix something like this on a kitchen table."

"We'll need traction."

"Okay, I'll have traction. Bring your gear here. I tell you, I'm having no nursing homes. I know too damn much about what happens in those places. Soft music laid on, but when you want a bedpan you can press a bell until you get a seizure. We'll drag Kirsty out and give her some work. Do her a world of good. Bring her back into the land of the living. I was once her ewe lamb. Before I started to talk."

163

I played mum at the tea tray while Archie prepared a hypodermic.

"I'm going to bed now," I said. "Anyone mind?"

No one seemed to.

It wasn't the sunshine that woke me up at eight, just a loud clang in the passage beyond my room. I was naked between sheets and almost at once wearied by the thought of trying to explain to Mitchell why my bags had been neatly stowed away in the cruiser I was using to rescue Angus. I needed a good story, I hadn't got one, and it didn't feel as though one was coming. After a bath I got into yesterday's shirt and, unshaven, went out to find what had been happening during the three hours of my sleep.

Angus was in the next room being attended to by a Chinese nurse his doctor had chosen with some care. She was well past her best, heavy and slow moving, with the look of a woman who has, in her time, fallen on more than one patient's appendectomy wound while changing a dressing. She stared at me with her mouth open, as though she found this place full of surprises.

Angus was trussed into a bed that didn't appear to be part of Ella's house at all, a rigid line of sheets across his chest making a grim neatness up that end. Lower down things were a bit different, a vast elephantiasis of plaster going up into the air via pulleys and a chromium steel support. Angus had his eyes open and they were bloodshot.

"You look horrible," he observed.

"All I need is a shave. When did Archie go?"

"God knows. I've lost all track of time. But it was a relief when he did. He brought that hairy ape MacGregor in for a consultation. At one stage I thought they were going to saw my leg off. It's about time you showed up. I'll have a lightly poached egg for breakfast. You're making it."

"Where's Kirsty?"

"She hasn't come out of her room yet."

"Where's cook?"

"He did a bunk after Tang. No, don't look at me. I had no contact with Ella's cook. He just got the feeling this wasn't a lucky house. So he took his wife and seven kids and father-in-law and left. Nursey here found out. She won't cook, she says. So unless you can get Kirsty on the job, it's you. Nursey wants her breakfast, too. Just a little bowl of chow mein with crispy noodles will do her nicely."

The kitchen door was shut, with Heather on the other side of it making the kind of noise a Siamese does when it's putting in complaints about the catering. I turned the handle very carefully. Kirsty had her back to me, with the fridge door open. She was dropping down bits of chicken and using baby talk to an animal which is always completely impervious to this.

"There, my wee pussums."

Heather swallowed and screamed again.

"Did my wee thing have to go with an empty tumtum?"

"I hope there are eggs because our patient wants one," I said.

Kirsty spun round. There was a fleck of chicken on her chin. She hadn't combed her hair this morning or put it in curlers the night before. It hung lank to her shoulders, and pink bald patches shone through from her scalp. She was wearing a faded blue dressing gown with tie cords, held together high at the neck by a tourist souvenir of bonny Scotland, cairngorm stones and mock silver thistle. She was an old woman driven from her cave of withdrawal by a rumbling belly and a howling cat.

"Did you know Angus was in the house?"

"I'm not caring who's in this hoose."

"Kirsty, we need your help."

"Who needs it? Who needs my help? You?"

"Angus."

"He's no bairn o' the Bains that. Just a wee tyke. And always has been."

"He's broken his leg. He's lying helpless."

"Why should I care? Who cares about me?"

"Ella cared about you. And I do."

"You? Would you make me a charity, then?"

"Kirsty, no one's making you a charity. You're going home to a life of your own."

"At my age? What sort of a life is that?"

"Wouldn't you like a house of your own? You're still a strong woman."

"Aye, I'm strong. But at my years you can waste. Especially when you're wantin' it. And I'm wantin' it now."

I didn't for a moment recognize the sound which came from her. I thought she was going to be sick. She moved toward a central table and sank down on a stool by it, putting her head on her arms. She was crying.

I set about making tea, smoking a cigarette as I did it. I gave Heather a wing to shut her up and found eggs. I can cook in a manner in an emergency, but out East we're still not used to doing it, and even remembering how to set about eggs and bacon was like going into a dark cupboard looking for something you haven't wanted in years. The fat I had in the pan started to smoke and go black. It smelled a bit, too.

"What's that you're doing?" Kirsty said at my elbow. "You're never using real butter for a fry-up? There's cooking fat, man!"

"I didn't see it."

"Oh, my goodness! Oot the way! I'll have to put this mess down the sink. You've wasted near a quarter of butter."

"The estate will stand it."

In fifteen minutes Heather was washing herself, the table was set with two places, and there were two trays. Nursey was going to have to like bacon and eggs.

"You take Angus his breakfast, Kirsty."

"No me. I'm not seeing him!"

I wasn't long in the bedroom, but when I got back Kirsty

was in blue serge again; she had washed her face and pinned her hair up into the usual knob on top. We ate in a silence that had a kind of genteel respectability about it, both of us wanting food badly, but watching our table manners like a couple of livers-alone suddenly forced into company and not wanting careless little solitary habits to show. I could have mopped up my egg with a piece of brown bread, but I didn't.

"The house'll be an awful mess," Kirsty said, rising. "Was it you that made tea last night?"

"Yes."

"You should never have used that Yokohama china. That's our best. Could you not see that?"

"I wasn't seeing much."

"And what have you been up to, then? I ken you weren't back here until late. With the police coming."

"It was pretty late."

"You could do with a shave. Did you fetch Angus?"

"Yes."

"I don't see why you brought him to this house."

"And yet you defended him in a way. You told the police he saw a lot of his sister."

"It was the family name I was thinking of. Nothing else."

"I see. You're remembering the inquest this morning."

"Aye. I'll be ready. Will you take me?"

"I will."

"There's time to do the sitting room first. I don't hold with the way these Chinese clean. And that Tang! I couldn't tell him a thing. He wasn't like the old boy we had. He'd call me 'Missie' and he'd listen. I made something of him, but not that Tang. I mightn't have been in this house for all he cared. I don't know what got into Miss Ella. I really don't."

"The cat wants out," I said.

"Aye. She didn't go for that pan in my room. Well, it's natural. With a beast."

No more pussums. I was glad.

Angus seemed much restored by bacon and eggs. I asked how he was and he said in agony, but I didn't believe it. We got rid of the nurse, and I shut the door on the sound of a vacuum cleaner going somewhere.

"Where did you get that nightie?" I asked.

"It must have come from MacAndrew's nursing home. It'll be on my bill. And it's a nightshirt. They facilitate the bed bath, friend. That hippo wanted to give me one, but I've postponed it. There's the whole morning to put in while you're away engaged by the due processes of the law. You hadn't forgotten?"

"No."

"What time do you go on stage?"

"Eleven thirty."

"Mitchell will be waiting. Rubbing his hands. You know he's right off me and onto you again. Everything ties up beautifully with his earlier theories. He's so happy about it all that it's quite made up for putting off arresting me. That's been referred up for a high-level decision."

"Congratulations."

"Yes, I'm quite pleased. They won't run me in, you know. Everything I said last night was the truth. And it all strengthens his case against you. He's sure now you came up here to stop Ella's money flowing in my direction."

"Ella sent for me, actually."

Angus dropped his cigarette. I had to pick it up from the carpet.

"The bitch," he said, as I gave it back to him. "She was hardening up. I could feel it."

"Hardening up from what?"

"One of her soggy states. They happened every now and then. May have been her liver. One of the first signs was her starting to yap about what is the meaning of it all. You know. The cure was whisky or another man. But latterly she hadn't been finding that either of these set her up. Hence the yoga, easing herself into another dimension or something. She didn't really believe any of it, but the bag of tricks fascinated her. I gradually eased her off that onto my project, sublimate in good works and all that kind of bilge. Which reminds me of a psychiatrist I knew who said he was for all religions because in their best forms they were excellent therapy. You know, I nearly spat in that smug bastard's earhole. Where were we?"

"You getting money from Ella."

"Yes. Well, I did. A lot of it. I used to meet her in a lousy coffee shop in Kowloon and pump in the tonic. But the surprise was really how easily the money came, knowing our Ella. Maybe she was really sick. But what did she tell you?"

"Practically nothing. She phoned me in Singapore and said it was urgent she see me. I had some business I could do and came right away. When I arrived off the plane we were social at once and stayed that way."

"And you never had a heart-to-heart?"

"No. We started to talk about you the night she died, and then stopped. There was something else on her mind."

Angus looked positively relieved.

"Something much more important than the money you were sucking out of her."

"Well, well," he said, looking at the ceiling.

"What I don't understand, Angus, is why Ella talked to you?"

"The answer's easy. The opportunity arose. There was a bottle between us, and Ella had drunk most of it. She had been keeping something to herself for much longer than is natural to any woman. And it had to come out. She looked at me through a blur and saw again the wee laddie she used to push in his pram through Broughty Ferry gardens. So it flowed out. All except the name. She wouldn't give me that."

"What did you say to your sister?"

"Why the hell should I say anything? I just listened. That's all she wanted. An audience for 'aren't I a clever girl?'"

"You didn't see any danger in what she planned."

"Hell, no. It never occurred to me she was up against a killer."

"This evidence you spoke about. You know where it is?"

"I know where I can lay my hands on it. But I don't have it myself, if that's what you're getting at."

"So you don't actually know who the killer is?"

"I'm a good guesser."

"I think you're a bloody fool. What you're doing is lying on a bomb right now. For your own health chuck blackmail and tell me."

"Look, Paul, I'm safer in this house than I would be in jail. And you know why? Because you're going to be here. After they've toasted you at the inquest the police are going to pop you back into Ella's nightmare and watch the place like a safe deposit vault. And here I am, tucked up with you. Cozy. I can wait while you play at being stubborn. You'll change your mind in a day or two and see things my way. You'll have to. And after all, the money I want doesn't mean a thing to you."

"That money is Ella's trust."

"Ella!" He leaned forward until the plaster cast wobbled. "A silly bitch who spent her whole life flapping about in a terror that she was missing something. She was like those women you meet who'll tell you after the third gin that they've never had an orgasm from their husbands. Junk! That's what they are. That's what Ella was. Sure, I used her. Sure, I'm sorry she's dead. It's the milk cow butchered!"

I went over and stood at the window. For a while there was silence. Then Angus said:

"Unclench your fists, friend. You can't hit a man in traction. You'll probably have a two months' wait. That is, if you haven't been hanged."

I went down to the jetty for my bags. The boat shed doors were still open, and the cruiser was still tied up at the pier, bumping its fenders gently against it. I couldn't leave a good boat like that exposed to a sudden southerly, and anyway I wanted something to do.

The cradle was still under water, which wouldn't be particulary good for it, but I switched on the electric motor in the shed and pulled the thing up into the shallows. I then untied the cruiser and eased it forward until it fitted snugly into its place on the cradle. When I got out to see that the craft was really balanced properly before the haul up, there was a policeman watching me from the steps. I went down into the cabin, got my suitcases from the locker, and set them on the pier. Then I used the electric motor and the boat came up, over the slipway and dripping, sliding neatly under cover. I closed the shed doors, hearing the lock click, and picking up my bags started for the steps. They were heavy bags, but the policeman didn't offer to help carry them.

11

The nice thing about an inquest is its basic informality. You deal with the fact of someone found dead under curious circumstances, in surroundings and in an atmosphere which rather suggest the annual opening of the flower show. Nobody is really accusing anybody of anything, and nothing exactly vital hangs on the proceedings. If the police are even mildly alert they have already come to their own conclusions and are busy acting on them. The coroner pretends to be in a position to be able to direct the commencement of an investigation, but he is really worrying about the recurrence of his dyspepsia. His dignity derives from a body which has to be buried and the fact that only he can issue the ticket.

There were a lot of pretty hats at the inquest on Ella Bain. The jury had three women on it, one of these Chinese and for once the worst dressed. She was a plump housewife who looked as though she had been dragged from her marketing and now believed she was on trial for murder herself. The other two women were dutiful citizens who had come, well corseted, to participate in a democratic process.

The men I didn't like at all. With one exception they were British business or civil service in a small way, conspicuous for their rectitude if little else. The one exception might, from his oily skin, have been a Chinese restaurateur, and he suffered from some form of nasal congestion which forced him to keep his mouth open throughout the proceedings.

We were in the kind of hall which exists in every town, village, and colony, and which might have Masonic connections, but is certainly used for the tennis club dance. There was room for a good number of spectators, and at this levee the crush had sent up the temperature by fifteen degrees even before anyone said anything. Two thirds of the room was filled by public benches with a clear space in front of them. Against the right wall was the jury, at a table at the top the coroner, and then to the left were chairs for the witnesses, who were neatly arranged in terms of their nearness to the discovery of the body. Kirsty was next to me, and beyond her, MacGregor, who sat leaning slightly forward with his hands clasped in front of him looking not unlike a television psychiatrist.

The coroner himself was a doctor in public health long since turned to cynicism by outrageous epidemics in the areas of his jurisdiction. This is the sad fate of many in the Colonial health service, and he had the fatigued voice of his disillusion. He was also rather slow about everything, as though any acceleration of the proceedings might allow something significant to escape. He opened the occasion by a somewhat lengthy peroration to the jury, indicating that a viewing of the body was neither practical nor likely to serve their purpose in being called. It was, however, their right to insist on this ceremony and they could do so, as he indicated, against his wishes. The jury decided to stay where they were.

Most variety performances offer the big names somewhere in the middle of the bill, but I was called first. There was a general murmur through the hall which suggested that everyone was pleased about this except me. I could never have been an actor and as a politician would have spent my career in the back seats, for I loathe an audience. I can never even look one in its corporate eye with that smooth assumption of public honesty which comes so easily to many a successful scoundrel.

173

After taking the oath I found myself with the coroner on my left, the jury straight ahead, and about two thirds of the hats and the gentlemen of the press over to the right. To say that I was aware of faces is not quite true. It was that corporate face again, many-eyed perhaps, but with only one identity and that hostile to me. The hostility seemed unanimous, and it came out as a kind of wave of suppressed aggression, repressed because everyone, including the Chinese, was British and believed in fair play. They only damned me, as they would have damned Bligh of the *Bounty*, to an honest trial.

The coroner led me—by what I felt to be a pretty clearly marked digression on my reasons for being in Hong Kong at all—to my discovery of the body. And during this question-and-answer game I found myself, with an almost horrible fatality, unable to look at anything but the Chinese restaurant keeper. The spell snapped only when he suddenly shut his mouth to avoid a circling fly and I was able to switch to the Chinese housewife. But her terror was so unnerving I was glad to get away again. Then I discovered that I could look at the press in anger, particularly after I spotted Asia New Light.

"Mr. Harris," said the Coroner. "You have admitted moving the body. It is very important for our purposes that we ascertain as nearly as possible the position of the body prior to this moving, and in particular the position of this remarkable collection of pillows in relation to the deceased's position in the bed when you discovered her. Can you in fact recall, Mr. Harris, whether any pillow or pillows were actually covering her head?"

"Not totally covering it. Because I saw her hair."

"You saw her hair. Now these pillows, Mr. Harris, this . . . ah . . . tumble of pillows."

He liked that. He had secret literary pretensions, like so many doctors and civil servants, and sent in cunningly illuminated reports.

"This tumble of pillows . . . were they in fact heaped up

174

behind the deceased? Or was she partially on top of them, with several thicknesses beneath?"

"I should say both. They were heaped up behind her, but I should think that there were at least two thicknesses under her head as well."

The pillows seemed to go on for a long time. The coroner very nearly had me guessing the number of them, like peas in a bottle, but I declined to do this. The police could count the things if they wanted to. I was then taken on a carefully conducted tour of my movements in Ella's room before and after using the telephone. Perhaps twenty minutes later, and upon signing my deposition, I was allowed to sit down, feeling as bruised in spirit as a schoolboy who has been forced into the recitation of the whole of Kipling's "If" with every hated word still seared on the memory.

Kirsty made a surprisingly brisk witness, with no wandering and not a hint of any home-cured opinions. She gave me a nod as she sat down.

MacGregor was something of a surprise. He answered all the coroner's questions about his action in the room of death, and then, just when he might have been allowed to sit down, he suddenly cleared his throat and said that in his view the presence of venous congestion and pink oral and bronchial froth did not point directly or necessarily indirectly at homicidal violence of one kind or another. There was no evidence of violence of any sort on the body, no contusions of a suggestive nature; and, while admitting that in the case of young children who had been overlaid there was often a marked absence of any pathological appearances whatsoever, he submitted that in the case of a full-grown adult who had been subjected to violence even while under the influence of a drug these would have, in some measure, been apparent, because a resistance of some sort would have been made.

The coroner seemed a bit reluctant to translate all this for the jury, but felt he had to.

"Do I take it, Dr. MacGregor, that in your opinion Miss Bain did not meet a violent death?"

"I'm saying, sir, that it wasn't necessarily a violent death."

"Thank you," said the coroner without gratitude. "Your little exposition indeed reminds us that it would be premature to assume a violent death for Miss Bain until the jury here has decided whether or not this was, in fact, the case."

MacGregor blushed. There was a titter as he came back to his seat, and my heart went out to the man. I was almost certain that he had made a misguided attempt to help me.

The Crown pathologist didn't share MacGregor's views at all and put forward a flatly contrary suggestion that the quantity of sedative intake almost ruled out the factor of physical resistance on the part of the deceased. The coroner liked the pathologist, but nobody else did. He was a dull witness.

During a duet for two slow voices I looked around the room. Like everyone else I knew that Ella had been murdered and this part could be skipped. Our audience was skipping it by staring at me. About a hundred and fifty pairs of eyes were plucking at me, including Diana Hisling's, from the middle of a row. The only person who wasn't focused on me was Wong, just along from Diana, and he was staring at her. I tried to find that interesting but somehow couldn't make it.

Archie took the stand after the pathologist. He gave his evidence as Ella's usual physician, describing her general condition, a slight cirrhosis of the liver and a noticeable enlargement of the heart, both of which states had been confirmed by the autopsy. There was no predilection to drugs, to his almost certain knowledge, though he had prescribed certain sedatives for asthma relief. The asthma was clearly attributable to psychosomatic origins and in his view was a direct product of tension. He had suggested psychiatric treatment which had aroused a certain hostility in his patient and he had not persisted in the matter. There had been a tendency recently toward an increasing frequency of these asthma attacks and they had become correspondingly more severe. Within the last month he had given his patient a specific diet which it was his impression she had made no attempt to keep to.

The coroner liked Archie.

"Would you give it as your opinion, Dr. MacAndrew, that your patient was an alcoholic?"

Archie considered this. Then he stated that while acute alcoholism is easily diagnosed, the borderline cases are not. There was no total abandonment to alcohol as a stimulus, though the use of it as such had been heavy and continuous.

It was a nice way of saying that Ella had been a boozer who didn't often fall flat on her face.

Mitchell was the star turn, an impressive witness who didn't follow any formula from the *Policeman's Guide*, looking at the coroner when he had to, but mostly concerned with the jury, who were now all sitting up straighter on chairs which were beginning to pain their backsides.

The inspector described how he had been summoned by MacGregor and had arrived to find the deceased in a locked room, her body as I had left it. He made a subtle point of this, not overstressing it, but the jury all looked at me again. So did the hats. So did Diana Hisling and Wong.

Mitchell went on to describe a painstaking and thorough search of the bedroom and the bathroom adjoining, suggesting the kind of microscopic carefulness which the public likes to expect from its police and then, without undue emphasis, stated that not a trace of any bottle or container of sedatives had been found.

The coroner interrupted. "You were particularly interested by this fact, Inspector?"

"Yes, sir."

"Is that because in cases where murder has been done there is sometimes a form of container left to suggest suicide on the part of the deceased?"

"That certainly happens."

"In this case it did not happen. What conclusions would your experience suggest from that?"

"It could be that the sedation had been administered before the deceased entered her bedroom."

The word "administered" was deliberate, and not missed. There was an odd sighing from our audience.

"Somnabin is not one of the quick acting sedatives," Mitchell went on. "I understand from inquiry and from the maker's label that the recommended use is from half an hour to forty minutes before retiring."

"From which you conclude that Miss Bain could have taken . . ." the coroner paused . . . "or had given to her, the sedation before going into her bedroom?"

"Yes, sir."

This wasn't nice at all.

"Inspector, did you carefully search the rest of the house . . . all of it . . . for any Somnabin container?"

"I did, sir. And found nothing."

"Is it a fact that this drug is easily obtainable over the counter without a prescription?"

"No, sir, it is not easily obtainable in that sense. Reputable chemists in this city would not sell it without a doctor's authorization. The fact remains, however, that it is available in certain areas and may be obtained by anyone who is determined to get it."

The coroner smiled.

"That would appear to be almost an indictment of the police, Inspector?"

Mitchell coughed, but it wasn't a spasm.

"For certain reasons our controls in this city are not totally effective. I would be the last to claim that they were."

Bluff and honest, that's what he was. The no-nonsense policeman doing a grand job against the obstacles to complete law enforcement which were obvious to anyone who lived in

Hong Kong. Mitchell would end up as commissioner, if he escaped lung cancer. And if he got me.

I was beginning to feel that the coroner had come to his solemn task with a mind already somewhat conditioned, possibly subconsciously, by a regular reading of *Asia New Light* in its original scandalous Chinese. The coroner isn't required to display the same almost innocent detachment from the real world which is expected of the presiding dignity in a higher court, and this one didn't. He hadn't liked my face, and his nose had twitched as he questioned me. Now he made a speech.

"Inspector Mitchell, it is not my duty or my purpose at these proceedings to in any way lead your statement to this court. At the risk of seeming to do so, perhaps, I must say that there is one matter which seems to me highly relevant to the question of how Miss Bain died, either by violence or by extremely exceptional . . . shall we say? . . . natural causes. We have Mr. Harris's statement that before he retired he and Miss Bain had one last drink together." The coroner smiled faintly. "Or was it only one? The time was early morning. You have suggested that Miss Bain may have taken the drug Somnabin before going into her room. Normally one expects a person taking a sedative to swallow the pills, followed by a draft of some liquid. It could perhaps be argued that Miss Bain, disliking the taste of this sedative in its prepared form, made a practice of dissolving the pellets in some type of imbibable alcohol. It might also be argued here that had it been the wish of any person or persons unknown to administer this drug to the deceased, a natural means of so doing would have been to put the pellets in a final drink. Do you agree?"

"I do, sir."

"In view of this then, when you were called to the house later on the same morning, only a few hours later, did you make a search of the sitting room for any used glasses left from this final drinking of which Mr. Harris spoke?"

179

"I did. When I questioned the houseboy I found that he had tidied the sitting room between bringing a breakfast tray to Mr. Harris and preparing one for Miss Bain. He brought this second tray into Mr. Harris's bedroom on Mr. Harris's orders. Mr. Harris himself then took in Miss Bain's breakfast tray, as we know from his statement."

"Quite. The houseboy had washed up any used glasses during his time of tidying the sitting room, then?"

Mitchell allowed himself his only dramatic effect of his testimony. He looked around the courtroom.

"No, sir." Another pause. "The houseboy Tang is most emphatic that there were no used glasses at all in the sitting room. He says he looked in the wine cupboard and found all the usual glasses there and clean."

The public benches had been quiet during the proceedings. They weren't now. It was much more than a sigh I heard then; it was a corporate gasp, followed by a rustling and the drone of whispers. The coroner pounded on his table.

Mitchell made no explanation of why a star witness like Tang hadn't been produced for the inquest, and the coroner didn't raise the matter. There might almost have been a psychic collusion between them.

The faces of the jury were not reassuring. They were ready now for the coroner's instructions, which they got, for no witness followed Mitchell. No more were needed.

My position was prejudiced, but I couldn't say that the coroner really slanted his summing up. He believed that Ella had been murdered and so did I. He went over the testimony brought before his court, for the most part without much comment and with only one salvo fired at MacGregor, who was, he pointed out, a general practitioner and not a medical scientist. The jury had to decide whether a grown woman, in moderate health, and even allowing for a considerable consumption of alcohol, could possibly turn her face into a pillow and suffocate to death. If this was not in their opinion either possible or likely, they must then consider how violence could have been done. There was absolutely no suggestion of any forced entry into the house, no trace of unidentified finger-prints around the door onto the balcony or anywhere in the deceased's bedroom. It would seem from this that the assailant, if one existed, must have had easy access to the house, and that this assailant's presence had caused no alarm. He had also to point out that there was no sign of any upheaval in the bed-room, nothing out of place, the wall safe untouched.

The departure of the jury gave us the feeling of being sus-pended in a vacuum. The coroner shuffled his papers, which included a huge plan of Ella's house to which he had never referred, blew his nose, wrote something with an automatic pencil, and looked impatient. Those at the back of the hall went out for air, and soon the rest of us heard them, through an open door, making it a social occasion, with talk released and little spurts of feminine laughter.

We heard something else, too, at least those of us in the wit-ness seats . . . the jury. The jury room was clearly the hall's kitchens, or perhaps the place where they dressed up the elves for the annual children's pantomime, and it seemed to be re-moved from us by only one door. Male voices predominated, and they were mostly drone, but after all of twenty minutes I heard a woman, a clear but shaky voice, and not British or happy with the English tongue.

"No murder, no murder!"

The coroner got that, too, his head jerking up. He signaled over a clerk. The man bent to receive a furious hiss and then went on creaking tiptoe from us. There was silence in the kitchens and the clerk came back, nodding to the coroner and posting himself by the door through which citizens with an awful weight of responsibility on them would soon be coming.

But they didn't come. The coroner, whom I wouldn't have thought a patient man except for his own deliberations, was soon clearly in a frenzy of irritation. It was understandable.

He had told the damn fools what to do. Why all this dithering about?

Members of the press, absent from the hall, kept popping back in to see what was happening, divided between a desire not to miss the verdict and the need for good camera stances outside. I wanted a cigarette badly and so did a lot of people. Only Wong looked imperturbable, his head bent over a book. Diana Hisling had gone.

The jury filed in after forty minutes, most of them hot and angry-looking. The Chinese housewife had been crying, and she was in the middle of the procession but spaced away from the others, as though a source of contagion. It was perfectly clear that somehow or other she had gummed things up.

It was clear to the coroner as well. At that moment he detested democracy. And when the foreman returned an open verdict I thought the poor man behind the desk was going to have a cardiac seizure.

Archie put his hand on my arm.

"Paul, we've got to go through that mob sometime. You'd think they'd have had their money's worth. But they won't go until you come out."

I smiled at him.

"It would be like missing the bride at the wedding. Archie, go on home yourself."

"What will you do?"

"Get a taxi. That's the way we came."

"There's no phone in this place."

"Well, send one back for me."

"Paul, I want you home with us. And if you're thinking about Louise, don't. It's my house. Look, I'll go out to the car and bring it to the gates. It'll take me about five minutes. You can run through the crowds."

"Towing Kirsty behind me?"

"Oh, hell. I'd forgotten."

"Perhaps I can help," Wong said at my elbow.

Archie looked almost angry.

"My car is parked in a lane," Wong said. "It's an Aston Martin and has quite a remarkable performance. There is a back way out. You have to push through a hedge, but that shouldn't trouble us."

"Thanks," I said. "Act as decoy, Archie. If you go to your car that'll hold them for a few minutes."

Wong smiled.

"I think if Mr. Harris meets the man from *Asia New Light* there will be another incident. Though perhaps you haven't seen that paper today?"

"I can use my imagination."

"I doubt if your imagination would be equal to it. We have no press council here, you see. At least, not one that covers our gutter news. It's . . . a remarkable story."

"Have they hanged me yet?"

"Practically, Mr. Harris. I would have thought that a prosecution of that paper is called for. But I doubt if one will be forthcoming."

"Paul," Archie said. "Have you thought about a lawyer?"

"Who's panicking?"

He looked at the floor.

"Hell!"

"The old lady is to come with us?" Wong asked gently.

"Yes."

He went over to Kirsty. "We're taking you home now," he said.

"Oh. Well, I'll be glad of a cup of tea. Oh, it's you, Mr. Wong."

"You remember me?"

"And why shouldn't I?"

"Chinese faces are all the same, aren't they? One looks like another. You can never be sure . . . if you're from Scotland?"

"We're not fools in Scotland," Kirsty said.

She found an umbrella as she rose.

The effect of Archie crossing the hall was what we wanted. The press cleared out in front of him. We waited until the hall was practically empty, and then Wong, Kirsty, and I went through the door the jury had used.

Wong must have done a recce of the situation. He led us down a stone-floored passage, past a room with tables and chairs, and out a back door. We walked over grass to the hedge, which I held apart for Kirsty. She didn't need help, hopping through easily enough.

There were no other cars in the lane at all, just the bright yellow Aston Martin. Even now I could look at a car and like it, but I think if I'd owned this job on the island it would have contributed toward a feeling of claustrophobia. There are only a limited number of places you can go, and the sleek little projectile would take you there too quickly.

We had a bit of trouble getting Kirsty and her umbrella into the back, and before Wong and I had slammed the doors the pack was on us, streaming down from the main road. I wasn't surprised to see Asia New Light in the lead, acting as his own photographer, his camera already held up.

The Aston Martin snorted, then went down the lane like something out of a sling. Asia New Light was well in our path, counting on Wong slowing and swerving, which would improve the chances of a good picture. The reporter had plenty of nerve but so did Wong, and he held the wheel steady, the yellow bullet not concerned with the death of a newshound as a by-product of its flight. My feet were hard on the floorboards when my scourge jumped back. Even then the car shaved him, and I looked round to see a camera lying in the road. We had no difficulty with the others.

"Thanks," I said, as we exploded past the crowd in front of the hall.

Wong didn't say anything until he was round another corner.

"Would you have done that yourself, Harris?"

"I'm not sure."

"You are sentimental about human life? You believe in preserving it when possible?"

"On the whole, yes."

"As you have seen I am not at all sentimental about Chinese. Only the Scots."

I turned my head. "Are you all right, Kirsty?"

"And why would I not be?"

"Why, indeed?" said Wong.

The hall was up on the Peak, in the heart of the residential area, and in seconds we were in quiet streets, the rocket motor scarcely grumbling.

"The Chinese are a superior people," Wong said. "But there are too many of us. Far too many. You can't feel part of such a mass. Or I don't. Perhaps it was a mistake to let me live in Scotland for so long."

"It's a terrible climate."

"Not at all. It makes you robust. All my family have died of chest troubles. Since Scotland I never even cough."

"It's still a wonder you didn't die there in the first year."

"Yes," Wong agreed.

After perhaps five minutes he said, "You've never used my phone number, Mr. Harris."

"I've scarcely had the time. But I'm extremely grateful for this."

"It's nothing; you should use me more. I was talking to a Mr. Li. In the film business."

"Oh, yes?"

"You picked up his wife, eh? She is lovely. But old now for my taste in entertainment. Still . . ."

"Mr. Li mentioned me?"

"Oh, yes. Many people do these days. He was distressed by your troubles. Interfering with your business."

"They have a little."

"Mr. Li thinks he might have backing for your Malayan silver. To what degree do you pursue business from your present circumstances?"

"I'll have a dictaphone in my cell."

"Open for business until the last minute. Good. We Chinese like this."

The road that went past Ella's house was empty: no parked cars, no policeman at the gates and no sign of one in the grounds as we turned into them. Kirsty went straight into the house, but Wong and I stood by the car.

"Can you sleep at nights?" he asked.

"You don't run the local agency for Somnabin, do you?"

He grinned. "I like you, Harris."

"You're now in the smallest minority with which I've ever operated. Except once in China."

"You won't ever hang."

"My lawyer in Singapore wouldn't agree with you. Though he does concede it may be a bullet."

"I don't promise that you'll die in bed. But you won't hang. On second thoughts we'll keep Mr. Li out of things. I'll form a little consortium of my own, with perhaps a million Hong Kong dollars to invest?"

I looked into his bright eyes.

"Mr. Wong, I've known one or two criminals who were excellent company off duty. I liked them in a way. But I wouldn't dream of doing business with them."

He didn't move. His voice was thin.

"Meaning?"

"Meaning that I have no intention of investing your Yellow Ox profits for you."

His face hadn't changed.

"That's slander, Mr. Harris."

"But not in front of witnesses. Thanks for the lift."

12

Angus would be lying in his bed panting for news of the inquest, so I didn't go to him; I took a drink out onto the terrace. The men who scrubbed the rocks appeared not to have shown up for work, and it didn't seem to me that this mattered at all. The view was still a Zen withdrawal from the facts of life: the carefully placed tree, the slightly phony ocean, and what looked like totally unusable boats floating around on it. Peace of mind was what this was supposed to offer. Like hell it did. If the stock market crashed and you were out on this terrace you'd still be thinking about how much money you'd lost since you went to bed the night before.

Kirsty brought me a tray with hot tinned soup and cold chicken and then, since it was about three, followed this up with a cup of tea and a Bain sweet biscuit. She'd already had a bang-up row with nursey and seemed to be coping quite happily with a servantless household, though I promised to try and find some more staff as soon as I could. She watched me sip the tea.

"I've been thinking, Mr. Harris."

"Oh, yes?"

"Miss Ella's in hell. And I'm on the road."

I very nearly spat out the tea.

"Sit down," I said.

Kirsty did so, rather carefully on the edge of her terrace chair, as though only the ungodly ever really relax into comforts offered.

"Now what's on your mind, Kirsty?"

"It was me that washed those glasses," she said.

For a moment I didn't quite get this; the sun had been making me sleepy. Then I realized she was talking about Mitchell's inquest bombshell.

"You did it? Why?"

"It's what I always did. I always went into the sitting room and tidied things up a wee bit, no matter what time it was."

"Kirsty, you waited up every night that Ella had a party or friends in?"

"Aye. Most times. I'm no one for a lot of sleep."

"But what did you do it for?"

"I didn't like Tang seeing the way things would be. I could see the smirk on his face when he went into the sitting room in the morning. It could be a right mess, I can tell you. But I should have told that judge."

"You could scarcely get up again after you'd given your evidence."

"Could I not?"

"The coroner wouldn't have liked it."

It occurred to me how much Mitchell wouldn't have liked it.

"Kirsty, you may have helped me. If I have to face trial."

"Is that what's going to happen?" She didn't sound unduly perturbed.

"It could."

"You didn't do it," she said.

The Harris team was getting bigger.

"Thanks. Any idea who did?"

After a moment she said, "How would I know? But what I do know is that there was a few who went up those stairs to her room. We played a game, Miss Ella and me, pretending I didn't know. It twisted my heart. But I didn't speak. She'd have sent me back to Scotland. She wouldn't be checked. It was her own way Miss Ella wanted. Even when she was wee."

"I see. Kirsty, keep quiet about those glasses at the moment, will you?"

"Is it right not to tell them?"

"It might be a great help to me."

"Oh. Well, maybe I'll not do it then. Though it's been on my conscience."

She got up.

"Are you expecting them to be coming for you for the jail, Mr. Harris?"

"Not quite yet."

I had a lot of sleep to catch up on and moved to a reclining chair. I wake when I'm stared at for any length of time. Archie was above me.

"Like a babe," he said.

"Hello. Been seeing your patient? How is he?"

"Feeling neglected."

"That's good for him. Sit down. What's the time?"

"After five."

"Like a drink before I consult you professionally?"

Archie sat on the balustrade.

"No. I've got to get on. What's the matter with you?"

"I'm all aches and pains. It takes me longer to get over a roughhouse these days. And carrying Angus didn't do my back any good."

"It's your years," Archie said. "Take a day in bed."

"In this house? It's no longer comfortable."

"Then come to mine."

"I'm tempted. Have me to dinner after a long soak in a hot bath?"

"God, Paul, you don't have to ask. Of course, come. I've got the nurse to stay on until I can get another to work shifts. Kirsty will be able to manage?"

"She's doing fine."

"We'll expect you about seven. Oh . . . I didn't see your police guards coming in. Where are they?"

"They weren't doing much good anyway, so Mitchell called them off."

"Isn't that a bit curious?"

"No, just Mitchell being cunning. He's luring me to use freedom. You'll find his men are behind bushes somewhere with a Jaguar hidden away. He's going to be saddened when I spend the evening at your place with my feet up. You don't mind plain-clothes men snooping about your house keeping an eye on me?"

"Not in the slightest."

I stayed in my bath for an hour smoking cigarettes and reading an article in an American magazine on what to do about crime in your neighborhood. Then I dressed with more than my usual care in a suit I had worn only twice before. As I walked down to the sitting room for a drink there were terrible noises from Angus's bedroom, his voice and nursey's, both howling. I didn't investigate, pouring my whisky carefully and turning with it to look about Ella's sitting room.

The place wasn't meant to have flowers at all, beyond a rubber plant or two, but Ella had disregarded her instructions here and gone in for three of those vast displays of bloom that are a morning's work for a lady of the English leisured classes. She couldn't have done these herself, but there was probably a flower shop downtown run by an English ex-lady who kept your house bright for a fat weekly fee. The lady must have been frightened off by press stories, for her flowers were now withered. At risk to my suit I collected them all up and took the heap to the kitchen.

Then I looked in on Angus, approaching his room through a stillness and finding him in the center of one, but in a rather tumbled bed.

"What the hell have you been doing?" Angus shouted.

"Resting."

He grinned. "The inquest really get you, eh?"

"Did you cross-question Archie?"

"Yes. It doesn't look nice at all. For Paul Harris. I liked the bit about the glasses."

"A triumph for Mitchell. But for his sake he'd better not build on it."

Angus looked suspicious. "Are you up to something?"

"Just taking it easy. What was the noise with your nurse about?"

"I've sacked her. I couldn't stand her any longer and said so."

"You mean she's left?"

"Yes. Cleared right out."

"Who's going to look after you?"

"Kirsty and you."

"It's a nice idea. But not convenient for us. I've just seen Kirsty and arranged for her to take the evening off. She needed to get out of this house for a while. So she's going to make the cat comfortable and then go to her friend who used to be Ella's sewing woman. A nice Eurasian lady. They had an evening together a year ago, and it's about time for another. I'm sure you wouldn't want to upset an old woman's outing?"

"And what are you dressed up for?"

"A quiet little dinner with friends."

"So . . . you're all just going to walk out and leave me alone?"

"How was I to know you'd sack the nurse?"

"Well, phone MacAndrew and tell him to get me someone else."

"I don't think that will be too easy. Archie said he'd just managed to persuade the woman you had to stay. If you will take things into your own hands . . ."

"I couldn't stand that monster a minute longer!"

"Then all I can do is make you comfortable before I go. Like the bedpan? I don't expect to be late."

Angus was breathing somewhat heavily. He reached out for

the phone. I got up and went over to the window, opening a long section onto a small balcony.

"A bit stuffy in here," I said.

He jiggled the hooks. "This line's dead!"

"Oh, I didn't want you to be disturbed so I switched the phone to Ella's bedroom. Mitchell still has the key to that for some reason, and he left the door locked. Who did you want to get in touch with? Lia Fan?"

He stared as I turned from the balcony.

"I can call the police in here!"

"I'm afraid they wouldn't hear you. Mitchell has withdrawn his men. It's quite a mystery move on his part, really, but there are certainly none of them about."

"What the hell is all this?" Angus asked.

I offered him a cigarette, but he made no sign that he noticed.

"I told you, Angus, I didn't like the feel of blackmail. A sort of taste in the mouth. Your turn to get the taste."

"What? You mean, you're leaving me in an empty house? With the windows open?"

"That's the idea. I'll close the doors. We don't want things to look too obvious. The position as I see it is that you're target number two for Ella's killer. I think he has this house under observation. He'll certainly know you're in it. I say 'he' but I'm not sure we can rely on that. There have been little feminine touches here and there. Like the tidying of my room to suggest I hadn't been to bed while I lay reeking in whisky. Could have been a woman. Even out on the island."

"You bastard!" Angus said.

"Who do you think killed your sister?"

"I'm damned if I'll tell you!"

"It may be your last chance to tell anyone."

"This is a bluff! You're not going!"

"How wrong you are. In about ten minutes you'll hear the mini drive off. I'm giving Kirsty a lift to her friend. I'll bring you Heather for company, if you like."

He pulled himself up in the bed, using his hands, as far as traction and that monstrous plaster cast would let him. Then he filled his lungs and bellowed, "Kirsty! Kirsty! Help!"

When that was over I said, "An interesting appeal to yesterday's sentiment. But I don't think you're going to find Kirsty responsive. And she's a long way off in a pretty well sound-proofed house. Putting on her hat, I should think."

He was being noisy about his breathing.

"You're not fooling me, Paul. The police are still out there somewhere, watching this house."

"I wouldn't say this house, though I agree they're still watching. But it's me they'll be interested in when I drive off. You said yourself that Mitchell had stopped paying any attention to you, so I wouldn't count on the police if I were you. In fact you've got no one, Angus, except me. Who do you think killed Ella? And where's that evidence?"

"To hell with you."

"I think the killer may well come by boat. The moon's late in rising just now. A little rowboat for a noiseless landing just down here somewhere."

"You're not scaring me!"

"I think you ought to be scared, Angus. I would be if I was lying trussed in a bed with the odds against me that are against you."

"You'd better go to your friends!"

"I'm on my way. I'll leave you with a little thought. It's something that would turn Mitchell's interest right back in your direction. You were in Ella's bedroom the night she was killed."

He had been sitting up almost straight, away from his pillows. Now he sank back into them, and fear was like a shout from his eyes, and lips, and hands tightening into covers.

"You couldn't leave Ella alone, could you, after I'd arrived? At any moment she might tell me all about your role as leech. And you tried desperately to get in touch with her. You were still trying early on New Year's morning. That was the call I took. Your parents should have seen that you got your adenoids out, Angus. You're a noisy breather. Somehow I didn't think Ella would take an adenoidal lover. She was catholic in her tastes but discriminating in certain directions."

"All right, what if it was me on the phone? You're just guessing that I was in her room after."

"I was guessing until I saw your face when I said it. I know, now. You must have been very close to the killer at one stage that evening. Even nearer than I was. He could have been down in the garden, just waiting for you to go."

"I don't want to hear any more of this. Get out!"

"Is that your final decision?"

"Yes!"

"All right."

I crossed the room, opened the bedroom door, and pulled it shut after me. But I didn't go away at once. After about a minute sounds began. They reminded me of the sounds a frightened child might make after the front door has been slammed by parents who have gone to the pictures, leaving only a night light burning.

Louise was being gracious under duress and staging this quite well in her own setting. The room was certainly her setting, everything in it making a quiet statement about her, and one or two not so quiet. There was the silver-framed picture on the piano for one thing—of a very much younger Louise wearing the Pocahontas headdress which proclaimed that she had been Presented at Court in her day, a not-very-shy-looking girl with three white feathers sprouting out of her head. No one had tipped Louise off that the top drawer didn't display those feather photographs these days. You might be persuaded to dig them out, with screams of laughter, but the silver frame on the piano was the wrong kind of advertising. There were, also, far too many roses in too many of those family heirloom silver bowls that can be bought at Sotheby's any time you have the money.

It was a restful room. That had been worked on for a long while, with an almost neurotic attention to neutral basic tones and subtle pastel shades to point them up. Even the roses were none of them the new hard colors, but faded tea elegance blown to that point of scented perfection where they were about to collapse altogether. Still, there wasn't a petal on polished woodwork.

Louise served the drinks in her room. She gave me a whisky that was certainly one of those brands reserved for export because you can't get Scotsmen to drink them, and it was watered into almost total oblivion. It surprised me a little that Archie accepted this dilute solution in his own house. But then, when he gave a party, his wife came as a guest.

"You must be frightfully tired, Paul," Louise said.

She was wearing green, a tone not bold enough to be called olive. The dress had been chosen for the room, not for Louise, and that's almost always a mistake.

"I had a good sleep this afternoon."

"Really? You mean when you got back from the inquest?"

"After Kirsty's lunch."

"The poor old thing! Whatever will become of her now?"

"She'll retire to Scotland and live another twenty years. Giving lectures to Women's Rural Institutes on 'My Life Amongst the Chinese.' With slides. And she's out on the town tonight. Visiting."

Archie looked up.

"Oh, Lord, I hope that doesn't mean Nurse Cheong is expected to cook? She won't do it. None of them will, and it's sheer hell if you ask them to make toast. Did Kirsty leave trays?"

"There was no point. Angus wasn't hungry, and I'm getting back early to boil him an egg. I'm afraid he sacked your nice Nurse Cheong."

"He *what?*"

"I think he called her a hippo in Cantonese."

"The bloody little fool! How easy does he think it is to get anyone for home nursing? I suppose he told you I was to find someone else? Just like that?"

"Yes, as a matter of fact."

"I'll tell Angus Bain a thing or two. He'll go into a nursing home and like it."

I laughed. "He won't like it. He'll spend all his time in your pretty rooms shouting that it's just another medical racket."

"If he takes that line he can get another doctor!"

"Archie!" It was a gentle rebuke from Louise. "You know you mustn't get excited just before a meal. And I think that's the gong now. Yes."

The Far East appears to offer the moneyed woman an easy life, and it does, up to a point. You don't have to actually do anything, but you ought to keep an eye on everything that is being done. If you leave all the thinking to your positive jewel of a cook, you don't eat all that well.

Louise and Archie didn't eat well at all. The service was good because the Chinese don't naturally trip over their feet, but the soup came from a tin and had been drowned in tap water. The homemade bread was sour, and the chicken had been a market leftover haggled about for three quarters of an hour before it was brought home and entered in the cook's "bookie" at three times the purchase cost. We had stewed Australian brussels sprouts with it, all this topped off by a pudding which tasted as though it had been steamed, in the traditional manner, in the cook's other socks. There was also an imported Stilton, wrapped beautifully in a napkin, but withered with age. The wine was Archie's, a hock embarrassed by the company it had to keep.

Back in Louise's room again, there was the problem of our evening ahead of us. My hostess wanted to listen to the late news, which she did, but there was nothing about me on it. I could see her nearly bursting to tell me that there had been, on the six o'clock version, but a look from Archie restrained her. She then showed me her latest water color because I had asked, even pressed, for the privilege.

Louise had got down to a basic realism in this work, possibly influenced by all those photographers in Hong Kong. It was the corner of a Chinese street, though I couldn't see her sitting at the end of it with her easel. Everything was there, including the washing hanging from an upstairs window.

"You'll be building up a wonderful record of your life here," I said.

That almost made her forgive me for being myself.

"Odd you should put it like that, Paul. I always say that some people keep diaries, but I have my pictures."

We then listened to the Grieg piano concerto on their hi-fi, which is a nice melodious piece even if a bit thin intellectually. I asked if they had *Fingal's Cave* but they didn't, so we heard a Californian soprano who had been raised on orange juice. After it Louise came up with the startling theory that a singer needed the sun to be any good. "Look at all those Italians," she said.

Next was a long player which started with *The Moonlight Sonata* and went on from there for another forty minutes. Louise listened to music in a manner which suggested it was piercing her like rape, lying back in her chair with her arms limp along its edges. She was certainly a long way from a pipe-smoking husband.

Then the phone rang, and she was up in a second. Louise was the phone-minder around here and there wasn't even a twitch out of Archie; he had been trained. The only thing he did while his wife was out of a room uncontaminated by the telephone was to get up and go over to lift a needle. She caught him at it.

"It's for you," she said from the doorway. "That Hisling woman. She sounded peculiar."

Archie made no comment. He shut the door carefully behind him. Louise, having decided to find me tolerable this evening, suggested that I go through the albums and select something to my taste. Her curiosity about what my taste would be was only faintly veiled, so I put on a selection from *The Mikado* and she smiled as though she had known all along. She sat down but kept her eyes open this time.

Archie came back looking troubled.

"I'm afraid I have to go out."

"It's always like this," Louise said, meaning that the world is always butting its nose into the civilized life. "I suppose it's Mrs. Hisling?"

"It is."

"Doesn't she know you have consulting hours?"

"She does."

A cold wind started to blow. I got out of my chair to "Three Little Maids from School."

"Archie, would you give me a lift to where I can get a taxi?" He stared.

"But you came here in the mini?"

"I know. And the watching eye was behind me all the way. I'd rather like to shake it off, if only for half an hour or so. I've something I want to do in town. I could pick up the mini tomorrow."

"No!" Louise said, as though the protest had risen in her and just popped out.

Archie looked at his wife.

"Why shouldn't I take Paul?"

"Because you can't get mixed up in anything! You've got your position to think of!"

"That's what you've been shouting at me for the last twenty years."

"Archie!"

They stared at each other. It wasn't a moment you could use to thank your hostess for a lovely meal. Louise swung

198

around and went to stand beside the hi-fi box which still had Gilbert and Sullivan bouncing out of twin speakers.

"This way, if you're coming," Archie said.

"Look, I'm damned sorry. I'll use the mini."

"You'll come with me!"

We went down a passage to his surgery, then out into a bricked courtyard with a high wall round it. There was a three-place garage and a black Daimler standing in the open, ready to be driven off. Archie ignored the black car, letting me into the garages through a hatch door. He closed this and switched on the lights. In here were a Triumph sedan and an M.G. sports. He patted the little two-seater on its green wing and looked at me.

"I got this to recover my twenty-year-ago youth. And guess what I found out? The toys don't give you that old feeling. I haven't taken it out for a couple of months. Shall we see if the engine's still working?"

"This car will rather defeat the point of my coming with you."

"Why?"

"I could duck low in the Daimler as we leave your gates. But they could see down into this."

"Not if you're under canvas," Archie said, unzipping the cover to his half of the seat.

"Looks pretty cramped down in there."

"What's the matter? Got rheumatics?"

I didn't think I was going to like the ride much under hatches. Archie opened the doors and started the car.

"Forgotten my medical bag," he said. "That's what a sports car does for you."

We were in the courtyard, with the engine shaking me, for about two minutes. Then I heard the click of Archie's feet and a gate creaking back. In a moment or two we were going quite fast.

"See anything?" I asked.

"A car up a lane. Could be a courting couple."

"Could be Mitchell's boys. Nothing following?"

"Nowt. Why did you jump up like a gazelle when the Hisling name was mentioned?"

"Did I?"

"Speak up, I can't hear you."

"I said 'did I?' "

"Yes, you did. Is it in your mind that Eric could have killed Ella?"

"There are a lot of things in my mind."

"He's certainly carrying on unlike Eric."

It seemed to me that Archie was shouting.

"How?"

"Not coming home to wifie, for one thing. Not like Eric, is it? He leaves the office at the end of the day and doesn't come home for rice and curry. Diana has it kept hot for three hours and then decides to have hysterics. I think you noted that she is more than slightly an hysteric subject. I do believe she thinks her man may have done something terrible like jumping into the harbor."

"What do you think?" I called up, beginning to feel the thumping on my backside.

"On the booze. Or possibly our Eric's got him a woman. That would be better for him than a month on iron tonic. There's nothing like a reconciliation after sin to perk a marriage up. And they've been rowing steadily since you sicked the police on them. Know that?"

"No, I didn't."

"Well, they have. Where is it you wanted to go downtown?"

"I've given that idea up."

"You never had it. You just wanted to come with me to the Hislings'."

"That's right."

"Well, this is a professional call. To administer kind words and sedation. And while I'm in there you stay under canvas. You're not snooping on my patients. I'll run you home after and give little Angus a shot of concentrated hell. I'm feeling in the mood tonight."

We drove for two minutes.

"Archie, why don't you and Louise break it up?"

"It wouldn't be good for my position. And that's a fact. Almost anyone but a doctor can get divorced these days. And some doctors. But not in my place out here. It would undermine my practice. Louise would see to that. She'd devote herself to it. She's told me. She wouldn't go home to England; she'd stay right here. With a purpose. She'd make a good job of ruining me, too. Louise has all the right connections. So that's my life, friend."

"You could make another life."

"Not now. I've got everything here I meant to have when I started out. It's been a long pull. I'm not chucking away what I've got. Not even to get rid of Louise. What do you suggest I do? Get a job as an M.O. on a cruise ship? Don't forget I've never been in the English health service. And even if I could squeeze in now I wouldn't much take to a salaried appointment in one of those godawful new towns. No thanks. What I have is a compromise, but it works. And with compensations. There's a line Louise doesn't step over often. If she does I blow up, like tonight. We're usually too genteel for words."

"Sounds hellish," I said.

"All right. An upholstered hell. Damn near the average compromise at my level, if you'll excuse the cynicism. I want most of what I've got in this town, and I'd like to see anyone try to take it away from me. Do I hear you muttering something?"

"No."

"I believe you used to like me?"

"Why past tense?"

Archie laughed.

"Listen, boy, what do you believe in?"

201

"I don't know," I said.

"Still adolescent. He doesn't know. It's a great big wonderful world, and he hasn't got the answers yet. I've got the answers, Paul. I don't believe in a damn thing except what I can hold between these two big paws of mine."

"Doctors get isolated early. They know less about living than they think. Perhaps that's why such a big percentage commit suicide."

"Yah!" Archie said.

We went up the sloping drive to the Hislings', right up to the porch.

"Have a snooze," Archie said, banging the car door.

I heard his feet on steps, then Diana's voice.

"Oh, doctor!"

"Has he shown up yet?"

"No. And I keep thinking I ought to call the police."

"Too soon," Archie said, and the front door shut.

I pulled myself out from under canvas. It was a dark night, the moon late or folded away behind clouds. But there was bright light from the front room, shining out from uncurtained windows onto a patch of lawn, the old lit lamp for the wandering boy. I felt sorry for Diana somehow, knowing that it didn't do any good to feel sorry for her. I got out of the car and went up the steps, but my eyes were down the sloping drive.

It seemed unlikely that we had been followed. Mitchell could, of course, have a watch on this house. I tried the front door, but it was locked. I went round from the shadowed porch, keeping tight into the walls. Someone was washing dishes in a pantry, singing a song from the mainland, one of Mao's songs. Probably the houseboy was a Red, waiting for the night of the long knives. He certainly hadn't locked the back door.

The singing was very near. I could see a moving, white-coated back as I edged past. Archie had left his medical bag

202

on the hall table. I could hear voices from the living room, but I had to go right up to the panels to make out words. Diana was crying.

"He said . . . he didn't want to live with me. . . ."

Archie was admirably professional.

"Mrs. Hisling, every marriage hears those words. They don't mean anything. Will you please sit down now and try to relax."

"But why isn't he back?"

"It's not eleven. The bars haven't shut."

"Are you saying that Eric . . . You don't know him."

"Any man can break out on occasion. Now I'm giving you a mild sedative. It won't knock you out. Just put things in perspective. . . ."

Snooper, that's what I was. It wasn't the first time, either. The cook-boy had changed his song. It was another of Mao's. I went to Archie's bag on the table and opened it. In the compartment on the lid, buttoned away, was an object one doesn't usually expect a healer to carry around. It was a forty-year-old Webley automatic with ammo clip attachment, an antique really, but still efficient.

13

Archie took the little sports car down Ella's slope and tucked it in close against the projecting shelter over the front door. He switched off the engine. I was sitting up on the seat now. The night around us was very still, no wind, not even a rustling. Archie was listening; we both were.

"Our arrival doesn't seem to have stirred up any interest," he said.

"Mitchell's boys are listening to music outside your house. That is, if Louise put the gram on again."

"It'll be on. She wallows in that stuff. I was wondering about Mitchell himself."

"I should think almost certainly at home for once. He has the dog-eared look of the family man."

"Got your key?" Archie asked.

"Yes."

The house was a sealed vacuum of dark, warm tunnels leading to catacombs of rooms. I heard Archie click the front door shut.

"Where are the damn switches?"

I found them. We had gentle lighting ahead of us, an easy lead-in to the high drama of the pink room.

"Rather heartless of you to go out and leave the little tyke. Or will Kirsty be back long since?"

"No. She's staying the night away. Her friend insisted."

I put on the sitting-room lights. The curtains in there were all drawn. I hadn't drawn them.

"Come with me," Archie said. "You'd better help decide what to do with our problem."

I went with Archie, down the passage to the bedroom that was beyond mine, one of the row of Ella's luxurious guest rooms, each with its own bath, and each different, offering an exclusive feature. I had the trained pine outside, Angus a balcony.

Archie opened the door.

There was one light on, at the bedside. Angus lay humped up against the pillows with his leg still hooked up high above him. The bed was tidier than it had been when I left. The curtains were drawn over the windows. I hadn't drawn them.

"Well, well," Archie said. "So you've sacked my nurse, Mr. Bain? Who's been looking after you?"

Angus didn't say anything. I had the feeling he couldn't.

"I left everything shipshape," I said. "Angus wants me full-time on the job."

Archie laughed.

"Need the bottle?" he asked.

Angus shook his head.

"Marvelous bladder control. Wish I had it."

He put his bag on a table beside the bed and under the lamp. I moved in quite close as Archie took a thermometer from his inside pocket. Angus opened his mouth and closed it again on the glass tube. For a wordy man he was certainly hugging silence.

"Pain?" Archie asked.

Angus shook his head again.

"Well, then, what are we going to do with you? Though perhaps the morning's the time to discuss that. And tonight . . . a couple of sleeping pills."

He opened his bag.

"But first, a little mild sedation for Paul here."

The Webley was in his hand, pointing straight at my chest. Archie pulled the trigger. Angus cried out, and I couldn't hear the click. Archie pulled the trigger twice again.

"I emptied that, you bastard," I said.

I heard the door opening, though I couldn't see it. Then Mitchell's voice.

"Dr. MacAndrew, you are under arrest for the murder of Ella Bain. . . ."

Archie seemed to hunch. Something was happening at the window to the balcony, the curtains moving. He saw that. He threw the gun at my face. It caught my ear. He got in the bathroom and slammed the door. The lock clicked. A woman screamed.

Mitchell and I hit the door together. It was a solid slab of stout wood with a good lock and didn't give that first time. Mitchell and I were in each other's way.

"Stand back!" I yelled.

The scream came again. Then it was cut off.

"It's Lia," Angus shrieked. "It's Lia in there! Get her!"

We got her, but not Archie. Glass shattered as the lock gave. Lia was on the tiled floor, crumpled on it. Archie had stood on the bath to kick the window open. There was a black square of night and a lot of glass in the tub. Mitchell began bellowing to his man to jump from the balcony. I left the bathroom and the bedroom, running down a corridor and then down the length of Yamabushi's star feature. At the doors to the terrace someone came in as I wanted out. The policeman grabbed at me. I hit him and he hit me back, a little man but with a well-packed punch. This put me almost back to the carpet.

"Damn you! The killer's getting away!"

"He's on the roof," Mitchell howled. "It's flat. I want torches on him from all round the house."

They forgot about me, which was pleasing. I left the room behind them but got into shadow before the torches started to come on. From the number of them Mitchell must have had fifty men.

I went down the path, Ella's steep path to the boat house, running again, stumbling only once. There was plenty of shadow at the top of those stone steps for all the illuminations behind. I waited, but not for long. The man coming wasn't using the path, but was detouring over all those rocks. The going made his breath loud. Then he became a shape against flashlight glitter. I should have kept my mouth shut, but I couldn't.

"You closed her eyes, damn you!"

Archie came at me. He had the advantage of the slope behind him and a good deal of weight. I was ready for that. But not for the thing in his hand. I didn't see it until too late. The blow I got would have cracked my skull if I hadn't jerked to one side. I took it on my shoulder. It put me on my knees, and I nearly fell forward from them onto my face. I put my hands out to save me; pain started to flame.

Archie was on the steps, with something he had dropped clattering down behind him, a metallic rattling. I couldn't run down those steps. I had to use the railing, holding on with one hand. The other wasn't a lot of use. The fingers wouldn't work. There was something broken up top, in the shoulder area, something sticking out. I was feeling more than a little sick.

The steel tube had a bend in it. I could feel that when I clawed it up in my good hand. I went on down holding the thing, about five feet of metal.

The boat-shed doors rattled back. I shouted, but I didn't seem to be in good voice. And they were making a lot of noise up at the house, those flashlights still playing games up to the roof. I went down, faster, but still having to grab out for the rail against dizziness. I was near the bottom when the electric motor for the cradle started up, a loud whine. Archie had yanked the lever round to full.

207

I made myself run along the concrete walk from the bottom of the steps to the slipway. It was the pier I was making for, to be on it when Archie came down from the sheds. It was his only way to the cruiser when it was launched.

Light came on from the boat house. He needed that light to see what he was doing now. It showed me the cruiser already out of the shed and coming straight down for me, monstrous, a juggernaut boat on grinding iron wheels. I think I cried out. I certainly stumbled and fell forward, dragging my legs up, curling my body off those rails. The enormous beamy overhang of the hull was above me for seconds and then passed.

I got to my knees and then my feet. Archie was running down the slipway. He saw me lurching up onto the pier, with that metal bar in my good hand. There was nothing in his hands.

He followed the cruiser, making a flying leap at it, grabbing the stern flagstaff. As the rails steepened for the last drop into the water he was lifted clear, his legs wriggling as he fought to pull himself up and over into the cockpit. He managed one hand on a seat back and began a slow lift. The cruiser smacked into water with a sound like cannon for a salute. Spray went up twenty feet. The boat slewed about, bow briefly toward the steps; then there was a kind of recoil from impact that sent the thing back toward the pier, stern first.

Archie was still just hanging on, his feet in the water. The violent lurch as the boat hit water had nearly shaken him off, and he looked exhausted. He didn't seem to see what was happening. There were seconds when I could have called out to him to let go. He might have saved himself. His head turned and I saw his eyes. Then he knew what was happening.

Archie's body was going to be the fender between a thirty-foot cabin cruiser and the jetty. He screamed. The boat ground him against stone.

I didn't shut my eyes. All I heard after the scream was the angry roar of the electric winch. The cruiser began to drift gently out again into the narrow channel, its planking saved by the thing plastered onto its stern. Then the body slipped down.

I don't know why I went into the water. But I dropped the metal bar and went down to the slipway, wading in, up to my waist, groping with my good hand. I found what I was feeling for and began a slow drag back up the ramp. There were suddenly a lot of people about. I wouldn't let them pull the body away from me and laid it down on dry concrete myself. He was all right from mid-chest up, lying on his back just like an ordinary dead man and with his eyes open, staring up at me.

I did then what he had done for Ella, perhaps for the same reason, a feeling that I didn't want his staring eyes following me down the widening corridor leading away from this moment. I bent over and used two fingers to pull down two eyelids.

The police surgeon used the pink room as a casualty clearing station. It wasn't the ideal place in which to have a broken collarbone set. Archie had hit me with a length of tubing used to hold up a beach umbrella. He had taken it as he came along by the pool. I didn't need to ask Dr. Ling what that blow would have done to my skull.

When my arm was tight packed against my chest in a sling I got a large slug of Ella's brandy, and a policeman was detailed off to see me to bed. The force isn't given any training in valet service and though my shirt had been cut off me and it was my left arm out of action, getting undressed and settled was quite a problem. My Chinese policeman wouldn't accept the simple solution of no pajama top and insisted on an elaborate chest protection which involved two safety pins.

"Sleep now," he said, at last content.

"I don't feel it coming."

"Doctor give you medicine."

"Ask him not to forget, will you?"

The medicine was two pills, probably police-issue aspirin. They didn't make me much less conscious of a broken collarbone or induce sleep. I lay in my dimly lit room while noise in the house beyond gradually quietened away into the sort of stillness in which I had left Angus earlier this evening. Nothing could happen, but the terrible quiet began to have a reminiscent significance.

I managed to undo the policeman's pins and, wearing only pajama bottoms and bandaging that somehow involved my neck, got out of bed. I paddled along in my bare feet to an open door which put bright light into the corridor.

Angus smiled.

"Well, if it isn't Christopher Robin," he said. "Do come in, sonny. Had a nightmare?"

"I haven't been that near sleep."

"If you think a collarbone is anything like a compound fracture of the leg, think again."

"You screamed for a couple of hours," I said. "I've only wanted to."

"A primitive nerve system is nothing to brag about. Peasants like you can chop off their hands and just giggle. Before you sit down, I need a bit of fundamental attention."

"Is no one looking after you? Where's Lia?"

"Mitchell took her away for questioning. You can't keep that boy from his routine duties. And a fat lot of good asking Lia things is going to do him."

"Is she all right? She was out cold."

"Archie hit one of those veins only doctors know about. She was active again in half an hour."

When Angus was comfortable I was about ready to sit down. He gazed at me.

"I hate to do this to you, but toddle along to the sitting room and bring us back a bottle of Scotland's wine of life. It's what we both need."

It was, too. Propped up on some of his pillows against the

footboard of his bed and using part of his quilt I was more at ease.

"Just one or two points," I said.

"I'm an open book. You've only got to turn the pages."

"Where did Lia show up from tonight?"

"From the cruiser. She'd been living in it."

"I put the thing away. She wasn't on it then."

"Did you look in the john? She was behind the door holding her breath."

"She moved into the boat after the police had searched it?"

"Exactly. A cold wait she had, too. She showed up here right after your mini drove off. You left the living-room window to the terrace open. Did you mean to?"

"Yes."

"I thought it must have been sheer viciousness. You're not careless. We had a lot of time, Paul, to do what we had to. Lia got the evidence first."

"You're rushing me. Where was the evidence?"

"In Kirsty's bedroom. The safest place to hide anything in this house. I didn't know where it was in there, and it took Lia three quarters of an hour. She says that room is something to see. Kirsty carries her total past around with her and crowds it into twelve by twelve of living space. But we had some things to go on. First, that Kirsty didn't know she was hiding anything, and second, that what we were looking for was small. Lia found it taped behind the drawers in a bureau."

"What taped?"

"A roll of recording. The blackmail instrument against Archie. Ella put her cute little machine in a bag and took it along, switched on, into Archie's surgery. He never guessed at the time, though Ella sent him a copy later. It must have been about the nastiest moment in his life when he heard the thing. It plays for five minutes, but it's a bomb with the fuse lit."

"Do you know when Ella sent this?"

"Sure. The day before she told me. About three weeks ago. She went on the bottle and waited. A trying time for my sister, waiting for his reaction. You see, the tape makes it inescapably plain that Archie first seduced Ella in his surgery. When she had called on him as a doctor. The fact that it wasn't all that hard to seduce Ella didn't make any difference. Not for Archie. On the tape she begs him to take her back, and reminds him of joys known and whatnot. It was all thought out. Very cunning. I haven't heard the thing but Lia has a good memory. She came in here looking sick. It surprised me. She's a strong girl."

I was feeling the way Lia had. Angus watched me.

"I never loved my sister," he said. "That's such a comfort at a time like this."

"Shut up!"

He didn't.

"Ella's ultimatum was simple. Archie was to divorce Louise and marry her. It would have meant his leaving Hong Kong. He decided not to."

"You don't have to go on."

But he went on.

"Ella could have put that tape in a deposit vault. But it was just as safe in Kirsty's room. And handier. No one would think of looking there. Archie didn't. Though he looked everywhere else. I suggest you add something to our glasses."

I did that. It took a little time.

"When did you decide to call in the police tonight?"

"About half past nine," Angus said. "Lia urged it and I was quite ready to give way to pressure. If it's any satisfaction to you, you'd scared me. How was I to know you were sticking close to Archie? What first put you onto him?"

"A bottle of whisky."

"Eh? Mitchell's going to be impressed."

"It's not something that would have stood up in court."

"Give."

"I brought Ella four bottles of my best. It's quite a good best, and I don't give it to many women. We weren't drinking anything else. The bottles were at the front of the cupboard. The usual branded stuff had been shoved well back in. And yet the bottle smashed by me after I was coshed was one of the branded ones. It had been dug out from the back. Not the sort of thing most people would do under the circumstances. They'd have taken the first bottle handy. But my visitor just couldn't smash that malt on tiling."

"Suggesting a Scots palate?"

"Yes."

"I might be said to have one."

"I didn't think you'd have been playing it quite so cool just then, Angus."

"Too true, I wouldn't have been. Panic has always been one of my troubles. It hasn't fitted in well with my new life of action. I should have gone after Archie out on Minshein instead of bolting from him. Still, I'm learning. I'll surprise myself yet."

I took a long drink.

"Tell me about Lia."

"Ah, now that's something to move to. How did I meet her? She was Archie's girl."

"She denies it."

"Oh, well, she'd stopped being some time ago. And women have to be allowed to eliminate chunks of their past at their convenience. But she was Archie's girl when I met her. Archie was helping me out, you see."

He looked at me for the surprise in my eyes he didn't get.

"Only sometimes. On the fringe of my game, you might say. Ready to answer an SOS though. He did a minor operation once out on Minshein. But it was Lia who really came over to me in a big way. We got her fixed up in this house. Ella was contemplating putting the screws on Archie, and she was in a mood to oblige on little things like that. And other things, too. In fact, Archie had quite a bit to do with Ella's money coming my way. He worked on her as well. I liked the man."

"You . . . liked him?"

"Surprised?" Angus smiled. "Why? Archie and I had a lot in common. Intelligence left us with nothing to believe in but still a primitive conscience that wouldn't stop wagging. Archie helped me with contempt for his own motives as he did it. I think I'm a chump, too. Maybe you could pin the humanist label on me. Humanism is nothing more than an old-time conscience wagging its vestigial tail. And there's a new crop coming along who won't have that stump to wag at all. It's going to be quite a takeover by the new man. He'll be gestated in technology out of Freud. You see the first of them about already. And millions are on the way. Personally I think it's probably a good thing there's a new ice age following up the new man."

I suddenly wanted to move around. I got off the bed. I could feel Angus watching me to the window. I flipped back the curtains. There was light out there, from a cold moon which had showed up late, when it was already sinking.

"Lia was Archie's lover. Was she yours, Angus?"

He laughed.

"Women want me as a little brother. I think it's a protection that's going to last me all my life."

"So she came into the refugee racket for the kicks?"

"Lord, no. Lia is a simple believer. A convert to a cause. Her dear sister got as far as Macao from Nanking, but couldn't get any farther. No money. So she threw herself into the harbor. Lia heard about it a year later. It makes her motives personal and real. Unlike mine. But I think I'll last longer. Where are you going?"

"Down to the boat."

"Like that?"

"No, I can manage trousers. And I'll get a sweater over my head somehow."

"Of course, that boat's your concern as executor."

"That's right."

At the door I turned.

"Angus, I think that subject to certain conditions I may make over Ella's money to you."

He laughed.

"This is where we ought to hear angel voices on the sound track."

He shouted after me, "If you'd like to hear Ella talking to Archie you can. Lia took a recording Mitchell doesn't know about. It should be in that cupboard next to the speakers."

When I got to the sitting room, bundled up with only one arm through a sweater sleeve, I looked over at the tape machine. But I didn't go near it. I didn't want to hear Ella talking to Archie.

The moon meant I didn't need a torch for the steps, but I took them slowly. The cruiser was secured all right, fore and aft, safe enough for the night, but still I went down. I wanted clear of Ella's house for a while.

I walked over the slipway and up onto the jetty and my feet in sneakers didn't make any noise at all. The boat just gave a slight sucking sound as I stepped down into the cockpit after untying her. The engine started at once. I ran, slowly and without lights, down the channel, out to a sea on which moonlight crackled over a breeze-roughened surface. I just kept the engine turning over, and we drifted from the point, away from a house with one light burning in it.

The cabin hatch opened.

"Can't a girl get any sleep?" Lia said.

I used my one hand to pull down a switch on the panel. Lia was standing on the steps wearing a great deal of ocelot, apparently as a nightie. She smiled up, though it seemed to cause her a certain effort.

"There's no need to look so astonished. This is my home at the moment. The police returned me to source and I just went to bed."

"Why didn't you come into the house?"

"I did, briefly, for this rag. Then I tiptoed out again. I've never spent a night in Ella's place. I prefer this. Someone else can nurse Angus."

"No one's doing it."

"He'll live."

"I'll take the boat in again."

"No!"

She came up. The ocelot was swathed around her like an Indian blanket.

"Let's anchor somewhere, Paul. And watch the sunrise. It can be nice in winter. And while we're waiting . . . you come below. It's warmer. I'm gentle with children and the walking wounded."